PUT TO THE TEST

BY DERRICK GIRARD

Contents

Preface:
When Success Turns to Frustration

You don't know how well you've been trained for life until everything you've learned gets put to the test.

My biggest test came a few weeks into 2020.

I had just finished breakfast with my two kids. My wife had left for work, and the kids were on the bus. I was starting to get ready to head into the office when I got a knock on the door. I opened it up and found the most regular-looking guy. I didn't know if he was going to give me flowers or a package, but it turns out he was serving me a lawsuit.

The thing was, this was my second summons in less than a month and the third in the past five months. When I took the official notification out of the process server's hands, I couldn't help but laugh. I bet he had never experienced that reaction before. He looked at me like I was crazy.

Why did I laugh? It wasn't a laugh of despair or devastation. If you knew me and saw me at that moment, you may have thought I was laughing to stop myself from punching a hole in the wall. But that wasn't it, either. I laughed because I was ready. I was prepared to take on whatever the world wanted to throw at me right then. If I had gotten another six summonses that week, I would have accepted them with a smile. I had already made the decision to fight, so nothing could come my way that could have pushed me down and kept me there. I was committed to an expression I've embraced as a lifestyle mandate: *Figure It Out* (FIO).

But as it turns out, that was indeed my last lawsuit. I am grateful for that. Because while I accepted my challenges with a smile, what was to come over the next weeks and months—and even years—was far from easy. I had some dark, difficult times. But I did what I had to do.

I had my smile on that day in 2020 because I had made a choice. I could have decided to fold up my tent and go home and let those who wanted to take advantage of me get away with it, but I didn't. I chose to stick it out. If I was going to lose everything I had built, I was going to be able to say I did everything I could to stop that from happening.

From Assets to Liabilities

I had spent the last several years building a company to solve what I saw as a glaringly obvious problem within the financial services market. I had been in various management and leadership roles in the financial services industry for most of my career, and I had learned that there was no way for advisors to communicate with their clients via text in a compliant way. As I learned more about this issue, I saw a huge business potential and decided to explore what could be done to solve the problem.

After I dedicated some energy to finding a solution, I realized the solution would require a software product. The problem was that I didn't know anything about technology. I went to my uncle, who happened to be a software engineer, and shortly after sharing my idea with him, we went into business together. We had a great partnership, with him focused on the software side while I focused on, well, everything else: Securing clients, operations, management, hiring, firing, legal contracts, lawyers, marketing, sales, and competitive intelligence.

The company was called ionlake, and the product was MyRepChat. I began to seek out clients from my professional network. After two grueling years of building the company, we were starting to get traction. Potential clients who had said "no" to us before (or didn't understand the potential of our product) began to come around and see what was possible when they integrated our technology into their business. We were starting to connect with some big players in the industry.

It's when you first get that hint of success that a target shows up on your back. Up until that point, my uncle and I had a great relationship. He was actually the only person in my extended family I still spoke to. My wife and I were close with him and his wife, and my kids loved hanging out with their uncle. I was the only family member invited to his daughter's wedding, and it was actually at that celebration (in October 2016) that I approached him with my business idea. But my relationship with my uncle was now starting to deteriorate.

My uncle did not have the business savvy I did. Even his wife admitted that. As the company grew, informal agreements about the business needed to be formalized. I was giving him advice the best I could, as was our company lawyer. However, he decided to seek out some external support through a regional business association. That's where he met a lawyer who saw an opportunity.

My uncle is a somewhat timid guy. So, this particular lawyer assumed I was too. He wanted to push my uncle and me around and, of course, generate some billable hours along the way. His attorney gave him bad information, which was no doubt influenced by receiving only partial data. Without notice, this attorney, on behalf of my uncle, began claiming personal ownership over the software owned by the company. I tried to help us work through these issues, but the tension increased by the day.

Then, one day in November 2019, as I was dealing with my uncle's nonsense, I got an email from a law firm offering to help me with my pending lawsuit. This legal trouble was news to me. I went online and made sure it wasn't a phishing attack. But it wasn't—it was real.

It turns out that another competitor was claiming patent infringement, which was just what I needed. This company had venture capital backing, so they had the financing to take on a rapidly growing competitor like us. Like my uncle's attorney, they thought they could push me around.

They were suing us in federal court. My uncle and I had actually reviewed their patent previously, and we felt confident we didn't infringe on it. But our opinion didn't matter at that point because we were now a party in a major lawsuit. As the owners of the company, we had to deal with this fight together, while at the same time, we weren't speaking to one another.

Their patent, essentially, boiled down to new terminology, not new technology. My uncle and I were able to build the technology as quickly as we did because the pieces to do so were readily available. However, their claimed invention suggested they came up with the idea of sending a text message through a virtual number and then sending that message somewhere to be archived. This was not new, and if you've ever used a Google voice number, you know this technology was not unique enough to have warranted a patent. But because the terminology sounded sophisticated and new, they claimed they had something original. The patent was granted.

Another reason we didn't think this competitor had a case against us: by this time, many companies were doing what we were doing, but the competitor didn't go after them for infringement. Our two companies competed regularly for clients; however, we both also lost clients to other companies doing the same thing. They only went after us. As I discovered, it was because we were the best of their competitors, and again, they thought they could push us around. They had financing, and we didn't, so they figured, why not try to scare us with a lawsuit?

But while we didn't have venture capital backing, my company had me, and I wasn't going to back down.

Never missing an opportunity, this lawsuit gave my uncle's attorney the feeling that he could add to the pile and take me down. A few months later, his summons landed on my doorstep.

What was the third lawsuit? Well, I had entered into an agreement with a private investor for a business loan in 2019—just as we were starting to hit our stride. But all the details hadn't been finalized yet. When things started going well for the business, his demands changed. I refused to give in to those demands. The investor and his young attorney, eager to prove himself, jumped on the lawsuit bandwagon like a couple of ambulance chasers.

In a few short months, I had to pile on the regular battles of running and growing a company with these three different lawsuits. I had a competitor trying to crush me, an investor trying to take advantage of me, and an uncle trying to destroy me. When these came up, I couldn't put aside everything else. I had to take it all on and Figure It Out.

That process server didn't just hand me a summons that day: he handed me the ultimate test. Was everything I was taught about perseverance, hard work, and dedication going to get me through to success, or would I falter and give up? Could I build a successful company while fending off attacks from all angles, or would I decide it wasn't worth the effort?

The battles I faced were so different, and each required its own unique approach. I had to compartmentalize not only how I handled each one but also how I engaged with our clients. I had to show up for my customers and staff, act like everything was okay, and then spend hours on the phone with lawyers to wrap my head around what was happening. We were in the middle of landing our biggest deals thus far, and I didn't want to mess that up.

I was like a duck sitting on a wavey pond. I may have looked calm on top of the water, but I was paddling furiously below. No one could see how hard I was working, but I had made a choice to keep things moving. So that's what I did, no matter what.

I was living on coffee and Nilla Wafers. I would wake up at four, three, or two a.m. sometimes and not be able to go back to sleep. Instead, I got on my computer and went to work. I essentially became a law student. I researched everything I could about our cases. I had to know what was going on. I knew if I wanted to win, I couldn't have someone else tell me what was happening. I had to understand patent law, ownership disputes, and investment agreements. I engulfed myself in everything I could to learn as much as I could.

Throughout all of this, I didn't let my family know what was going on between my uncle and I. They all loved him—especially my kids. I didn't want my business issues to influence their relationship with him, and I was hopeful he would come to his senses.

Of course, this made me go through a lot of extreme emotions. I was able to present myself as a calm duck to my staff and customers, but at some points, furious paddling crept up above the surface. At home, I had a short fuse. I got angry. I was easily excited.

My wife and I both work very hard, and our careers are very demanding. Our two children, Nolan (at the time, ten years old) and Olivia (then seven) were just like every other kid. Sometimes, they test your patience. Sitting at the dinner table one evening, after a difficult day dealing with lawyers, trying to understand the absurdity of the scenario I was in, my son chose not to eat his dinner.

This was not uncommon, but today, I was in no mood to have the argument one more time. I lost my temper, I yelled, I smacked the table, and I made both my children cry and my wife angry by how I chose to react to what was going on beyond the dinner table. I felt like I was losing control of my business, and that caused me to be unable to mentally handle losing control at the dinner table—even if it was just over a piece of broccoli or some pasta.

These are the moments that happen during extreme stress. No one can be a robot during these times. Emotions will come, and they must be dealt with.

But I pushed through. All of my hard work was just about to pay off right before everything fell apart. I just had to persevere a little longer. So, I did.

Habits of Perseverance

All of my training was put to the test through these lawsuits. I had to call on so many different aspects of what I had learned growing up as an Army brat, through my time in the Air Force, as a financial advisor, as an executive, a public speaker, and as an entrepreneur. I realized that the habits I had internalized would help sustain me throughout this challenging time.

Too many people have not built these habits into their lives, keeping them from success; however they define it. I have met countless people throughout my life who are quick to give up or blame others. These are not people who lack intelligence or don't have the ability to succeed. They just do not have the habits required to persevere through challenges.

Success comes from hard work, and luck is a part of it, sure, but I have never met anyone who has achieved big things without getting up every day and pushing through whatever challenges they may be facing at the time.

Life is not an easy path. We all face challenges, either personal or professional, by just walking out the door and being a person. When you add on the pressures of trying to create something or achieve big things for yourself, that path gets even harder.

But if I could do what I did—taking on three different lawsuits at the same time while also growing a company and being a good father and a good husband—you can take on whatever challenges you are facing. I am nobody special. I am just someone who understands what's required to pick yourself back up when you get knocked on your ass, even if you keep getting knocked back down over and over.

Throughout this challenging time, I never had a specific moment where I sat myself down and said, "I will Figure It Out." There was simply no question that I would. It's just how I am wired, how I approach everything in life. Only after I was through the tough times was I able to look back and see what I had built into my day-to-day life that allowed me to survive and keep moving forward.

This book shares all the habits I've internalized as I developed this Figure It Out mindset—or what I call the "FIO mindset"—and the habits I've seen in other successful people as well. These habits can help you work through whatever comes your way. I know because I've lived with them and seen what's possible.

This is not a self-help book. It's not a feel-good book. I'm not going to tell you, "Anything is possible if you just do this or do that."

No, this book is about doing the hard work that is required to get anything done. I want you to understand there are a handful of very simple things you can do for yourself that can put your life on a better path than the one you are on now. These habits are as applicable to growing a business or fending off a lawsuit as they are for advancing your career or helping you create a better relationship with your family.

All it takes is a little perseverance. It costs nothing and is available to everyone. You just need to have the right training.

Introduction: Why You, Why Now

If you picked up this book, you are probably going through something like I was. You may not be in court, but you have some kind of challenge that has you stuck. You feel like you hit a plateau in your personal life, work, career, or business, and you can't get past it.

Long before my lawsuit challenges, when I first started my company, I faced a challenge probably relatable to anyone starting a company. The first call I ever made to promote our product was to a very small financial services firm. I got right through to their compliance officer, and we had a wonderful discussion about how the product could help them solve some of their problems. The conversation went very well, and we scheduled a time to talk again so that I could demo the product. Coming off that great call, I made the obvious next step: I picked up the phone and called the largest financial services organization in the United States and one of the largest in the world.

Yes, I was that arrogant. And stupid.

I was lucky enough to connect with someone in the right department, but they were not the right decision-maker. The call, overall, was positive, but it didn't lead anywhere. In the coming months, I would call over and over again, send email after email, asking for a meeting with the right people, only to be constantly brushed off.

Finally, I learned the real roadblock I faced: they didn't need my product. This company, with its deep pockets, told me that they were going to build their own product instead of using one like mine. I was devastated. I had worked so hard to build this relationship and show the value of what we built, only to get nothing. But I knew that if I was going to be successful, this wasn't going to be the only obstacle like this that I would face.

Of course, the obstacles we face are not just professional or related to growing a business. Maybe you are like my friend who met his wife late in life. He was single until his forties. He married a woman who already had a couple of kids. Once they got married, they decided to have a kid themselves. This was a guy who had been on his own for so long—and now he had four other people depending on him, all day, every day.

He loved this new life, but it was hard. He was used to being able to get up and leave when something wasn't going his way. Not an option anymore. He had been completely set in his ways, and then his ways dramatically changed. He didn't know what to do.

Or maybe you are like a former friend of mine who decided, after years in the corporate world, to go out on her own and start an insurance business. She wanted a new challenge and the freedom and flexibility that came with it. Insurance sales is a tough industry to go into—you have to dig deep into your social and professional network to find clients, many of whom might already have a relationship with an insurance agent.

My wife and I wanted to support her, so we switched over a few of our insurance products to her and the company she represented. After we signed the deal, I didn't hear from her for a few months, which didn't surprise me, as I assumed she was working her tail off. When I finally ran into her out shopping one day, I asked her how the business was going.

"Oh," she said. "I had to quit."

I was shocked to hear this but not really shocked to hear why. She had so many reasons why she couldn't make it with her new business: The economy was terrible, no one would return her calls, people did not want to buy insurance right now, she didn't get enough support from the insurance provider, and on and on. She had so many excuses as to why it didn't work out. Instead of learning from these challenges or even anticipating them in the first place, she gave up.

Maybe you're like another friend of mine who struggles to stand up for herself. One time, this friend needed to buy a new car, and she decided she was going to go to the dealership all by herself. Of course, she got talked into all the extra crap and add-ons she doesn't need. Maintenance packages, dealer insurance, clear coat, and the list went on and on. She told me the story, and I asked her why she had just gone along with what the salesman suggested.

"I don't know, Derrick," she said. "I'm not you. I guess I just needed someone like you to be there with me."

But here's the thing: she did not need me to be there with her. No one needs a Derrick to follow them around and fight the battles for them. I'm no one special.

Everything I was able to do—fighting off three separate lawsuits while building a business and being there for my kids and wife—I did because I didn't give up. It wasn't easy. In fact, it was quite hard, but I had already built the habits to keep me going. **Success doesn't require extraordinary people to do extraordinary things. It just requires ordinary people who know what they want and not giving up until they get it.**

I'm not talking about seeking out fortune or fame or awards or anything material like that. In fact, if what you are after is something that someone else has to give you, and you can't achieve it for yourself, put this book down right now. This isn't about that. If you want to ask the universe to bestow something upon you, there are a lot of books that will attempt to convince you that positive thinking or a strong enough desire can make things happen. This isn't one of those books.

This book is about one thing: persevering through the hard stuff of life by Figuring It Out. By the time you finish the last chapter, I'll guarantee that you will know exactly what you need to do to overcome whatever challenge is holding you back, whether it's adjusting to a new type of family life, overcoming a business challenge, or not getting walked over all the time.

Not through any tips or tricks but by getting down to it and doing the work.

Quitting—The Easiest Thing to Do

When I tell you to think about the movie *Jerry Maguire*, what's the first thing that comes to your mind?

I'll bet it's a four-word phrase: "Show me the money."

That line came from the character Rod Tidwell, played by Cuba Gooding, Jr., a football player and client of the main character, sports agent Jerry Maguire, played by Tom Cruise. If you can't remember the plot, Tom Cruise decides to go at it alone and start his own agency. He does it in a dramatic moment—yelling out to his entire office, "Who's coming with me?!"

The only people who do go with him are Renée Zellweger's character and Cuba Gooding, Jr. as his only client.

Everyone remembers the "show me the money" scene.

But that's not what that movie is about. It's not about the money. It's about the risk Tom Cruise takes when he goes out on his own. And the risk those that follow him take.

Jerry Maguire could have been a movie about a guy who stays at his job and does just okay. But that wouldn't be a very good movie. In the end, Tom Cruise does end up showing Cuba Gooding, Jr. the money, but that's not what makes the film exciting. It's exciting because Tom Cruise takes a risk, and we don't know what's going to come from that risk.

There's no reward without risk. Tackling risk requires hard work, and the bigger the risk, the bigger the reward. Have you ever known someone who takes a trip to Vegas with aspirations of winning "big"? When they return, you ask them how they did, only to learn they stuck to the penny slots the entire time. No surprise they didn't win big. You aren't going to win "big" on those machines. Maybe you'll get a few bucks here and there. To have the chance to win "big," you have to be willing to play the games with "big" payoffs. These games, like craps, have more risk with a bigger chance of losing but a bigger payoff if you win.

How many people aren't giving themselves a chance because they are playing the wrong game?

The easiest thing to do is to walk away from something because it's hard, risky, or scary. So many people do this, not knowing how close they could have come to success. They give up on their dreams because they can't stick it out. But the truth is: if it's worth it, it's hard. Everyone wants to achieve big things, but to do that, you have to do the work. Don't expect that slot machine to make you a millionaire.

Sometimes, when I'm talking to people about the value of the FIO mindset, they assume I am talking about buckling down and gritting through any challenge that comes your way. Never quit, ever.

But that's not it. Tom Cruise quits his job to follow his dreams and start his own firm. That was the right call for his character in that movie. Not quitting the job would have meant quitting on his dreams. If you are stuck in something, sometimes quitting is the hard thing to do *and* the right thing to do, so you don't give up on what you want out of life. If you have big aspirations, you have to warm up to the idea that it's going to get uncomfortable.

But what keeps people from pursuing what they want or leads them to quit before they get a head? In my experience, it's one thing: fear.

Fear of failure, fear of what others think of you, or even fear of success (yes, there are people who are afraid something might actually work out). We don't want to deal with the fear that comes up when we consider what is possible. It's scary, I know. Fear keeps people from doing a lot of really smart things.

In fact, some people may be unwilling to find their way to success because it goes against their own notions of who they are. People like to make excuses, like my former friend who tried to start the insurance business, rather than acknowledge they can achieve something if they work hard enough. Sometimes, it's easier to tell yourself, "It will never work," over and over, rather than accept you can be something more if you just try harder.

I tell my kids: excuses wake up ten minutes before you do. When your alarm goes off, the excuse will be right there, sitting on that snooze button. You WILL want to tap out. There are hundreds of reasons you can tell yourself that that's okay. But you can't. Setbacks are still steps forward if you choose to view them through the right lens. Giving up is a lousy alternative to admitting you may need some help. The reality is you are going to get knocked down again and again in life. You've got to learn how to keep getting back up, and the only way to learn that is to go through it.

Continuing to do something that doesn't make you happy and doesn't lead to success is the exact wrong thing to do. That's avoidance. That's insanity. We need to cut out all the BS in our lives and get to the things that really matter to us. We can overcome the things that hold us back from that true, meaningful level of success.

Finding Your Challenge to Get to Success

Before I can help you achieve your version of success, we need to identify what's holding you back. I want you to have one specific challenge or barrier in mind as you read through this book. It can be big or small, personal or professional.

You could be at a different point in your life and have to do a few things in a different way than you have done before. Maybe success came easy before, and you have hit a point in your career where you can't get ahead. You could be that sales guy who was so good that he was promoted to manager, even though he didn't know anything about managing other people and is now struggling in this new role.

Maybe your business was going great, but you were doing so well that now competitors have popped up, trying to take you down. Some customers are leaving you, and you haven't had to fight as hard before.

Or maybe you are like my friend, with a new family. This brings a lot of joy but also its own challenges. You have to navigate the people in your life in a way that's completely different from what you did before.

Basically, you are going through a midlife challenge and don't know how to get on the other side.

Notice I don't say "midlife crisis" here. You could be going through one of those, but again, that's not what this book is about. Midlife crises are about identity and what "you" means to you. This book is about overcoming something you are facing that is *new* to you based on where you are at in your life. You don't even have to be that far along in your life to experience this "midlife" challenge— I was in my thirties when I went through my first major challenge with lawsuits. I expect to live long past my sixties.

Instead, think of it as a midlife "wall" that you are coming up against. The wall may have always been in front of you, but for a while, it was far off, so it didn't bother you. Now, it's getting closer. Maybe you've already slammed right into it. This book will give you the tools to climb over and keep on going.

You may have a challenge on your mind as you're reading this. You know exactly what your wall looks like.

Or maybe not. You may just have a general feeling of being stuck. That could be because you don't know your challenge, or you've got a lot of them. You could be like my friend who always gets up-sold into stuff she doesn't want, with a personality or personal traits that keep holding you back.

Here are a few questions to think about to help you figure out what's your "wall" or maybe refine the barrier a bit:

- Do you have a personal relationship in your life that's very meaningful to you but has become challenging? Is this something you want to improve or walk away from?

- Are you struggling with how your career is going? Do you want to advance in your career or maybe consider a career change?

- Do you want to start your own business or take on an entrepreneurial project? Is this something you've always wanted to do but haven't been able to commit to?

- How are you doing at your current job? Are you performing at the level you'd like?

- Do you have an athletic or physical goal you want to achieve but can't reach that milestone?

- In general, do you feel like you are progressing in life? Or do you feel like you have plateaued in certain areas?

Remember—what's on the other side of these challenges shouldn't be fame or fortune. Overcoming the "wall" is all about personal fulfillment. You can't dictate what others give you—only what you give yourself. The habits contained in this book will help you control yourself and your actions, no one else's.

<u>The Hurdles Keep Coming</u>

After I got rejected by the largest US-based financial services company, I could have decided to move on. Heck, since we were still so new (and had such little revenue), I could have even chosen to shut the business down completely. Instead, I chose to Figure It Out through what I call *professional perseverance*. I stayed in contact with this company while we were both building a competing product. I even stayed in touch with thousands of advisors at this organization so they would know what we were doing. Then, one day, my phone rang. They told me that I was being invited to one of their corporate offices in North Carolina for a meeting to discuss my product.

I put together a small presentation as a follow-up. In my first slide in that presentation, I had a picture of a huge hurdle, something like fifteen feet tall. I looked out over the conference table of the half dozen or so people who could make my company successful with one decision and said to them, point blank:

"You approached this problem all wrong."

Remember when I said I was arrogant?

I explained to them how they were approaching the product as one giant hurdle. They asked themselves one question: *Could we build a tool to allow compliant texting?* Simple question, simple answer: YES.

What they didn't know (but I did) was that the issue wasn't just one big hurdle. Their one simple question actually led to many, many more questions, which would lead to even more hurdles. *How can you make the tool user-friendly? Will there even be a need for this tool? Can it integrate with existing software?* Each question presents further hurdles to jump over. There were thousands of hurdles in front of them, but they just didn't know it because in life, and in business, you can often only see the one hurdle in front of you. The harsh reality is you will never know how many more hurdles there are.

"I've been jumping these things longer than you have," I told them. I showed them my next slide, which was a field full of hurdles. "You can definitely catch up to me, sure, but what will that cost you? And what will you lose as you wait around? How many of your competitors will start to use my product?"

What I meant by this was that this company was going to need to put in the work. To make this product successful, they'd have to overcome a new challenge each day. There was no doing it once, and then it's all good. I knew it would be a grind because I was living it. At the conclusion of this meeting, they realized I was right.

It's the same with life. You may think that you'll overcome some big challenge, and that's it. You are good from there. But that's not reality. Success isn't an achievement. It's a process. It's the way you set your life up. It's how you put in the work.

Just by reading this book, you have set yourself up better than most everyone else because most people do not want to put in the work.

This book won't give you the tools to jump over the highest hurdle you can think of because that one hurdle that leads to success doesn't exist. It's in your mind. Instead, you need to prepare for the field of hurdles that are before you. You need the strength and stamina to keep up, and you need to know how to attack each one.

For that, you need to create some habits. That's what you'll get by the time you finish this book.

Chapter 1: The Fundamentals of Figure It Out

Takeaways:

- Excuses don't solve problems.

- The only choice you have is how you can Figure It Out.

- There are two essential mindsets that humans can adopt: A *fixed* mindset and a *growth* mindset.

I became the man of the house in third grade. My dad, and by extension, my family, was stationed at Fort Hood in Texas at the time. When you think of the American military, Fort Hood is what comes to mind. The base is approximately a quarter of the size of Rhode Island. The base, the surrounding towns, and basically the whole state of Texas was entirely in support of the military. We lived in a military bubble—maybe the biggest US Military bubble in the world.

After a few months on the base, my dad got the news he'd be deployed in support of Operation Desert Storm. He was infantry at the time. He shipped off, leaving me with my mom and two sisters. This wasn't anything new to us: we had moved from a base in Alaska to Fort Hood. At this point in my life, I had already lived in California and Germany as well. It was just the way our life worked.

When he returned from overseas at the end of the operation, my dad had more news for us: we were moving to Panama. He was going to train and lead other infantrymen as a jungle instructor.

Panama was not like Fort Hood. In both places, we lived on military bases, but in Texas, we had that supportive bubble. We did not have this in Panama. We were moving there on the heels of Operation Just Cause when American forces removed that country's dictator, Manuel Noriega. Some Panamanians were still Noriega supporters or generally did not like the American interference. Americans were not well-liked, the country was very poor, and violence towards Americans was constant.

Panama has now become a huge tourist destination. But back then, I was never permitted to leave the base, and any travel my family did between bases was done without stopping. Looking out of the windows of those military vehicles, my sisters and I could see the sandy beaches, palm trees, and oceans that now bring people from around the world. But we never got to experience those off the base for ourselves.

My dad traveled ahead of us to the base, so my mom, my sisters, and I flew together to meet him. We got off the plane, and my mom had to find my dad, who was meeting us there. She took my two older sisters and left me with our pile of luggage. This was long before cell phones, so I had no idea when my mom would be back or if she had found my dad.

We had shipped most of our things from Texas to Panama, but they were all caught up in customs. Sometimes, the customs process took months, so this luggage was all we had at the time and might have been all we had for a very long time. I had learned not to get too attached to possessions because, in moves like this, some boxes never show up. If they do show up, it's been so long you forget what you even packed.

As soon as my mom and sisters left, I realized how much this place was not Texas. There I was, this blonde-haired, blue-eyed kid who spoke no Spanish, sitting on top of a pile of luggage, just waiting. I was on high alert, wishing that I had at least backed our luggage up to a wall. People were swarming around me, and I was expecting one of them to try to come for me or take some of our stuff. My father had told us about the tensions in the country, and I was preparing myself for anything that might happen.

It was clear to everyone that I did not belong. I remember thinking: *If someone comes for our stuff, I'm going to go down swinging.*

Having to get physical was not something unusual for me. As I was growing up in a military family, tensions would run hot, and my parents would sometimes get physical. Expectations were especially high for me, and when my father would ship off somewhere, he'd remind me I was the man of the house. I knew I had to be ready if someone came for me. Luckily, that didn't happen, and we all made it safely to the base. But at that moment, as a ten-year-old on top of my family's luggage, I had to ask myself a few questions:

Did I ask for this? No, I did not. My dad's career brought us here. My mom had left me to watch the luggage.

Did I have a choice? No, I did not. Someone had to stay with our stuff. I don't remember why it was me, but knowing who I am, I probably volunteered.

So I decided: I've got to Figure It Out.

It wasn't the situation I wanted in my life right then, but it was the situation I got. I could have complained to my parents and whined, but it wouldn't have done anything. Any typical kid would respond this way, coming home one day to find out they are moving to a new town, much less a new country. That child would beg, cry, and plead to stay in a comfortable and familiar environment. But in my case, when the military tells your father he needs to relocate, there is no negotiating. We were moving to Panama and that was that.

The only choice I had was how I could Figure It Out. The only way I was going to get out of this situation was straight through it. Just like with my lawsuits, just like any other challenge that would come my way throughout my life. I had to deal with it.

That was the first time in my life that I saw the value of perseverance. My response to the situation was to stick with it, and I got through it. We had a great time as a family in Panama, an experience most other families don't get to have. I made many friends fast because everyone there was also going through the same thing I was. Military bases are some of the greatest melting pots of people because diversity (although that word is never used) is everywhere. None of us knew any better, and we all lived the same life. This was before the internet and cell phones, so all we knew was what we experienced. For us, it was constant change.

After Panama, we moved to a base in Chicago. Even though we were back in the US, Chicago was similar to Panama in that we weren't really welcome outside the fence. The base was next to a not-great neighborhood, with a lot of gang violence, near the suburb of Waukegan. Our backyard backed up to the nonmilitary parts of the Chicago area, with nothing but a chain link fence in between. There were numerous shouting matches between me, my friends and trouble on the other side. Threats were made. I was still this blonde-haired, blue-eyed kid, but now a little older and bigger—fourteen years old, five foot seven, and one that would not be pushed around.

I stood up for myself, no matter what. But when you stand up for yourself and *by* yourself against gangs, that's a bad place to be. I was dealing with a lot of guys who thought they were tough and wanted to intimidate me. But I wasn't going to let that happen. In Panama, I might have gotten into a fight or two, but I didn't have to worry about drive-by shootings.

Once again, the reality of the situation was very clear: My parents had to be in Chicago, and there was no version of me that was ever going to be a pushover. It seemed it would only be a matter of time until my mouth and my approach to standing up for myself would get me in trouble. My parents had to choose how to respond.

The choice was simple: they got me the hell out of Chicago. I went to live with some family in Minnesota.

This approach to life was ingrained in me so young that I did not even realize the habits it created until I was put to the ultimate test with my business. When I was stuck with a challenge or in a situation I didn't want, I didn't make excuses. Instead, I asked myself: *Did I ask for this? Did I have a choice?* No? Then, let's move on.

The only useful question in life, no matter the issue, is: *How can I Figure It Out?*

If your spouse is having a bad day, what can you do? You can talk about your bad day, or get angry, or ignore it, or you can choose to be a supportive partner. You can sit and listen while preparing a nice meal with a glass of wine to help them take their mind off the day. Or you can choose to unload about your day and play a game of one-upmanship about who has it worse until someone gets upset. What's the best choice there?

Or if a competitor is coming hard for your business, how can you respond? You could complain about how it isn't fair or begin bad-mouthing the competition. Or you could double down on your work and make sure every single person knows why your company is better than any competitor.

A friend of mine applied for a new job at her company. This new job would come with a raise and more responsibilities. She was clearly the most qualified person within the company for the job and interviewed very well. She was convinced the job was hers.

What happened? They brought in someone from the outside. Even worse, my friend was the one to train this guy into the role. She was pissed.

What I tried to help her see was that maybe *she* thought she was the best for the job, but those hiring had a different idea about the role. She was technically very skilled, but the other person had more "people skills" that, in some ways, cannot be taught. They may have decided that these intangibles were better than what she had to offer.

You may be pushing for a promotion at work, but your boss doesn't think you are ready. What can you do? Complain to your colleagues? Or worse, stop doing the work that needs to get done? Or can you figure out what to do to get ahead and then do it? This means you have to wait until the next promotion opportunity, but at least you have learned something and will be more prepared next time.

Another thing I learned on the military bases of my life, both as a kid and later when I joined the Air Force: excuses don't solve problems. You must adapt, Figure It Out, and overcome it. So many people learned the opposite in life. When faced with a problem or something that doesn't go their way, their go-to is excuses and blaming.

Excuses are easier and, far too often, not questioned. "I didn't get the job" is justified by accusing the company or interviewer of something rather than acknowledging that maybe someone else is more qualified. "Coach doesn't play me" is justified by accusing the coach of favoritism rather than acknowledging that maybe your attitude or work ethic is poor. "I'll never be successful" is justified because of someone's social status rather than attitude and mindset.

People learn to make these excuses, to give up—in big ways and small—rather than continuing on to achieve their dreams.

Instead, we must adapt and overcome or even step up when no one else wants to. Shortly after September 11, 2001, when I was in the Air Force Reserves, my base sent out a request for additional security help. I signed up, even though it was a scary time in America, and it would completely disrupt my life. I knew it needed to be done.

Don't rely on excuses. Determine how you should Figure It Out, then do it.

The Perseverance Mindset

Carol Dweck, a Professor of Psychology at Stanford, has found that there is one major quality in a person's life that can lead to success. It's not the amount of money they have growing up or their connections in life. It's their mindset.

Dweck discovered that there are two essential mindsets that humans can adopt: a *fixed* mindset and a *growth* mindset.

If someone has a fixed mindset, that means that they believe their abilities are fixed at a certain level. They have a set level of intelligence or physical strength.

This doesn't mean that these people think less of themselves. In fact, it's usually the opposite. They believe they are the smartest in the room or the strongest on the team.

By contrast, people with a *growth* mindset believe that almost everything about themselves can change. They can become smarter, faster, and stronger. They don't worry about whether they are the smartest in the room because they know it doesn't matter who is smartest—that can always change.

Guess who tends to be more successful? Those who absolutely *know* they are the smartest in the room, or the people who are willing to work hard to become the smartest in the room?

Dweck and her colleagues found that "it's not always the people who start out the smartest who end up the smartest." Instead, you have to work for it.

One of my best friends from high school excelled at every sport he played. He won awards and was even voted "Most Athletic" our senior year (I was, of course, voted class clown). He earned himself a full-ride scholarship to a prestigious university to play football, but after just one year, he transferred out. He said, "Coaches don't play me enough." He then transferred to another university, and wouldn't you know it, they also didn't play him enough. So, he transferred one more time, and the same thing happened.

He was used to being the best athlete in the room. When he no longer was, he struggled to learn how he could be better; he tried to change the room. His talent wasn't enough because, the hard truth was, his work ethic was inadequate. He expected success in his current environment simply based on the success he had in the previous one, rather than having to work for it. He was accustomed to being held up, not picking himself up.

People with a fixed mindset tend to be more willing to give up on problems or avoid them altogether. Those who see things through a growth mindset persist through challenges and do not give up, always looking for opportunities to learn.

In other words, they Figure It Out.

Other researchers have built on this "growth" mindset concept to figure out how the way we think about ourselves helps us lead successful lives. Angela Duckworth, in her book *Grit*, looks at how children can benefit from a growth mindset combined with a commitment to perseverance. She says that we can achieve our long-term goals through "passion and perseverance." If you give up on your passions, you aren't going to achieve your goals.

The right mindset is the first step, but a mindset is nothing without actions. People assume they need to take big steps to become successful, like jumping over a big hurdle. But that's not what life is. It's a series of small hurdles.

That's what this book will give you: the habits you need to build to take the right actions for success.

About 40 percent of our actions are habits—performed in the same way in the same situations each day. How we think about our lives drives these automatic behaviors. We can have a growth mindset and choose habits that help us to persevere, or we can have a fixed mindset and choose habits that lead us to avoid problems or make excuses.

Often, we let the desire for a certain fixed goal prevent us from creating the habits that can help lead to our success. I had a friend who was out of work for over four years. He had gained a lot of weight. He knew what he needed to do—get in shape. But he couldn't get himself to the gym because he didn't know where to start when he got there.

He thought about the problem as a giant hurdle to overcome rather than a habit to form. I told him, "Don't worry about what you are going to do when you get there. Just get to the gym and start."

Marathoners will tell you that the hardest mile is the first one. If you have some kind of goal fixed in your mind, you'll be too afraid to get started. But if you just put one foot in front of the other, you'll eventually get to where you are going.

Define Your Own Success

If you are good at sales, landing deals may seem simple. You pick up the phone. You talk to people. You do what you do.

But that process is never easy. You have to learn how to be good at sales, and you learn by doing. Pick any cliché you want about success and perseverance— "Picking yourself up by your bootstraps," "Pick yourself up, dust yourself off"—saying those things is easy. But actually, doing them is hard. To use another cliché; it is easier said than done.

However, perseverance does not always have to be hard. It's not always comfortable, it's not always easy, but it's also not always hard. When you have learned how to sell, the process becomes simple. You don't have to literally grit it out, exhausting yourself each day to get what you want. In fact, doing that is probably the quickest way to burn yourself out.

No matter how hard or exhausting it is, perseverance should always be simple. Simple enough to write a book about it to help you build your habits. Instead of trying to achieve dozens of things, you can just focus on one habit at a time.

First, you have to have your own definition of success. How you persevere depends on how you think about what you want to achieve. This could relate to the challenge you thought of in the last chapter, or it could be bigger than that.

Again, simple is better. Mine is that I always want to be able to say "yes" to my family. If my family wants to take a vacation, I don't want to have to say, "Sorry, we will need to save for years to do it." I grew up with a lot of "no's" in my life. I want to live a life of "yes."

That definition gave me permission to push myself and work harder. Importantly, this definition also allowed me to have a growth mindset. There was no real endpoint to my success. It was about a state of being.

I didn't say, "I want to be more successful than my sibling or neighbor," which I know is a lot of people's definition of success, even if they don't want to admit it. That's a fixed definition of success, always defined externally. Think about it: if your brother is a loser, do you think you'll become a doctor? If your goal is simply to be more successful than your brother, I don't think so. You are just going to work a little bit harder than your brother.

There's a difference between the standards you set for yourself and the goals you want to achieve. You can have high standards for how you want to live your life, such as living healthy. This is about what you will accept and what you won't. Then, you set a goal for how to achieve those standards. You can say you want to live healthy, and then your goal is to lose a certain amount of weight.

Because of the standards you set, you can't make your goal dependent on what other people think. I doubt you'll succeed if your goal for losing weight is to "be skinny" or to "be attractive," which has nothing to do with your internal standards. Maybe you'll lose some weight right away, but if you don't keep up the habits, those pounds will come right back. But if you want to get off your blood pressure medication, that's a goal with a clear standard, which leads to definable steps that will always push you to persevere.

I was in the Air Force Reserves in college to help me pay for my studies. I did not want to go into debt, and my military background made it a natural fit. One day, in my sophomore year, on a Saturday, while at the mall with my college roommates, I got a call telling me I had to pack my things and report for active duty on Monday.

Did I ask for this? No. Did I have a choice? No. So, all that was left was for me to choose how I could Figure It Out.

My goal at the time—my definition of success—was to graduate college in four years. I was not like my friends, who were on the four-and-a-half or five year plan and mostly seemed interested in partying through college. I saw college as a way to get my degree and get my life started. I knew I wanted to own a business, so I majored in Business

Management with a minor in Business Administration. I would later add Financial Planning once I discovered my passion for it.

I had no desire to hang around more than I needed to. I paid my own bills and made my own food. I didn't go home and have mommy and daddy do my laundry. Many of my friends did not seem like adults. They seemed like children living away from home.

When I got called up, my goal didn't change. My objective was still my objective: graduate in four years. I had to make some adjustments to reach this goal, including taking classes over the summer and maxing out my available class load each semester to stay on track. But I stayed on the same path with some slight detours.

Getting to that degree in four years wasn't easy, but it was simple. I knew what I wanted to achieve, and I did what I needed to do to get there.

The Habits of Figure It Out

A lot of motivational speakers work to make you feel good about your life or inspire you to dream big about things. You leave those sessions—or put down those books—feeling like you can take on the world. But ten minutes later, what do you actually remember from those speeches or those books? What do you actually change in your life?

Because if you don't change anything, how can you expect anything to be any different?

To persevere, you have to be able to adapt to your environment. My wife jokes that you can throw me anywhere, in any situation, and that I'll be fine. I can talk with a plumber or a CEO; it doesn't matter. I'll make a connection with whomever. I credit my military brat upbringing with teaching me this skill. All the moving we did forced me to adapt pretty quickly to any environment. I continued to ask myself those two important questions: *Did I ask for this? Did I have a choice?*

You don't move from Alaska to Panama and still wear your parka. But most people expect the environment to adapt to them. When it doesn't, they complain. They make excuses. Instead of asking, "How can I Figure It Out," they ask, "Why is this happening to *me?*" As if anyone cares.

Sometimes, you do have to change your environment. Leave a bad job and get out of a bad relationship. I'll talk more about this later in the book. But sometimes, you have to be comfortable with being uncomfortable and doing what is necessary.

In all things in life, we have to take responsibility for our actions. There are negotiables, and then there are non-negotiables. Don't confuse the two. Everyone wants to negotiate the non-negotiables: The kids who won't listen, the boss who doesn't think you are as brilliant as you think you are, the competitor who didn't get the memo that you're the only business allowed to go after these clients. Assignments with deadlines are non-negotiable, taking care of your body is non-negotiable, and providing for yourself and your family is non-negotiable.

But there's nothing you can do about those things—there's no shortcut for hard work.

Instead, you have to Figure It Out. That process is a combination of perseverance, dedication, and knowing what you want and why you want it.

So, what's that look like? Figuring It Out can be broken down into twelve different habits:

1. **Motivate Yourself**: If you are looking for validation somewhere other than yourself, you're not going to be able to keep going. You need to know yourself before you can achieve any goal.

2. **Be Self-Aware**: Know your strengths and your weaknesses. Be honest about both. That's the only way you'll be able to build a successful life.

3. **See things in Black and White**: Don't live in the gray area—commit. The gray area allows you to adjust your outcome to fit the habit rather than the other way around. Black and white holds you accountable for adjusting the habit, not the desired outcome.

4. **Don't Take "No" for an Answer**: Professional perseverance is a cornerstone of success. If you want to achieve something in business or your career, you can't give up. You have to be respectful and have patience.

5. **Forget About Your Goal**: Do not worry about achieving some intangible end goal. Instead, build in regular practices that lead to your definition of success.

6. **Be Humble**: There is no way you are the smartest or most successful person in the room. Be humble and create that growth mindset in yourself.

7. **Get Good Training**: When a Navy SEAL was asked why they train so hard, he replied, "Under pressure, you don't rise to the occasion. You sink to the level of your training." We never achieve anything major without first getting the training we need.

8. **See Opportunities**: If there's a challenge or unsolved issue, see it for what it is: an opportunity. Solving problems you didn't know existed can help you achieve what you want to achieve.

9. **Recognize Luck**: Sometimes, you get lucky. Don't pretend like it's anything other than that. Use it when you get it, but be prepared for when you don't have it.

10. **Persevere with a Purpose**: You need to know what you are suited for. If something's not the right fit, sometimes sticking through it is the exact wrong choice. Get direction to keep you from blindly moving through life.

11. **Adapt and Move On**: Don't create excuses. Create solutions. When you are presented with a problem, don't dwell on it. Move past it.

12. **Teach Your Children**: What we learn as children influences who we become. Be a model to future generations and teach them the habits of perseverance.

Throughout the rest of this book, I'm going to walk through each of these habits, chapter by chapter. Don't see these habits as a checklist in which you need to complete everything. Since you know your situation or midlife challenge from the last chapter, you can pick out some habits that you think may help you get past it. Parts of all of these habits will help you, but there are probably a few that stand out as priorities.

For example, that friend of mine in his forties who is struggling with a new family may want to focus on number seven—Being Humble—or number nine—Seeing Opportunities—to help him accept that he now has dependents and can no longer come and go as he pleases.

Or the friend who got oversold at the car dealership may want to focus only on number ten—Persevere with Purpose—or number two—Be Self Aware—so she can identify in which situations she may need to ask for help— and not get talked into a list of extra purchases that were not necessary simply because she didn't have the confidence to stand up for herself and say "No thank you."

Pick a few of these to start and see where that work takes you. Because this book isn't about a quick fix—it's about application. You won't see me smiling at you on stage, telling you to 'think positive.' This book is for people who want to work hard. Maybe you've fallen back on excuses before. After you read this book, you won't have any excuses for using excuses.

You can create day-to-day habits that help you persevere through the good and the bad, the challenging times and the times of triumph. The rest of this book will walk you through each of these habits and how you can apply them to your life.

Chapter 2: Look Inside Yourself

Takeaways:

- Motivate yourself through your own desires and goals for yourself, not anyone else's.

- Don't seek external validation for your choices or how you live your life.

- Find accountability partners and the people who will help you achieve your goals.

At the height of my battles over the three lawsuits, my wife saw me inhaling those Nilla Wafers, climbing out of bed at all hours of the night, waking her up. She kept asking: *Why? Why would I keep putting myself through this?* Without explicitly saying it, she wanted me to throw in the towel, and I can't blame her for that.

If my life were a movie, this part would have come about thirty to forty minutes in when things aren't looking great for the main character. There would be lots of shots of me staring off into space or at my computer screen, looking increasingly frustrated. Maybe I'd hit a punching bag until it fell to the ground.

Usually, in those kinds of movies, the main character has a wife or girlfriend who comes up behind him to give him a back rub or offers him a beer to ease the stress. These small acts serve as a moment of calm in an otherwise stressful time.

In the movie of my life, my wife and I did not have these kinds of interactions during my lawsuit battles. My wife and I are very open and honest with one another, probably one of the main reasons we've been together since high school. The idea of starting and running a business scares her. When I shared with her my idea of the business, she supported me, but the idea and the risk were something that made her very uneasy.

My wife and I have always agreed on the "why" of our lives. Even without discussion, we both are very clearly aligned on working hard for our family. To help put our kids in a great position to succeed in life and for us to have the things we want. However, my wife has always been frustrated by how I've chosen to pursue this "why." She is not as comfortable taking risks and would gladly exchange some upside potential for any form of certainty.

When I got served a lawsuit not once but three times, it would have been very easy for me to back off, fold up shop, and not continue with the business. I could have achieved our family's "why" with a different "how". But I didn't. As time went on, the fights got harder, the stress got higher, and my wife disagreed more and more with my commitment to this "how".

In her mind, I didn't need to keep doing this to myself. In my mind, I didn't have a choice.

Did I like what I was putting her and my family through? Of course not. I wish it hadn't happened. I wish things went very differently, and I didn't have to do what I did. But I had no other choice because I knew myself.

The first habit of perseverance is to look inside yourself to find your own source of motivation. I start with this habit because so few people consistently do this. Instead, they look to others as a source of their motivation. There's nothing wrong with wanting or needing a support system in your life, but that support system isn't going to point you in the right direction for you.

When you face challenges, you have to make the right choices for yourself and only yourself. No one can take on your challenge for you. Only you can keep yourself going down the path towards what you want to achieve. If you look elsewhere, you are likely going to end up failing.

A support system can help keep you going, but it can also help you convince yourself to give up. If I had done what my wife and many other people wanted, I wouldn't be where I am today. You need to learn how to use your support system to achieve your own goals—not to choose what others want you to do.

Find Your "Why," Internally

If you look outside yourself for motivation, all you are going to find are excuses to fail. Or someone who will tell you it's okay not to reach your full potential.

There are so many great examples of people who had every reason to fail. None more so than myself.

Throughout my educational career, I went to twelve different schools. In my senior year, I was voted not only as the "class clown" but also as the "teacher's worst nightmare." I barely even graduated, and that's not an exaggeration. I had no idea if I was going to make it out of there. My GPA was less than 2.0 on a 4.0 scale. When I did graduate, I had no plans to attend college.

Why would I? Neither of my parents attended college—my dad had a GED, and my mom had a high school diploma. Both were long-haul truck drivers, my dad moving into this career once he retired from the military and my mother following him into it. My older sisters did not pursue any education beyond high school. Most of my extended family consists of blue-collar workers.

No one would have questioned me if I had settled down and accomplished nothing with my life after high school, given how things were going for me at that point..

To be clear, blue-collar work is essential, respectable labor. I know many, many blue-collar people who have done very well for themselves. One of my proudest moments was when I was working on my sister's house, and her daughter's boyfriend couldn't believe that I had started a tech company and wasn't a contractor.

My point is that no one told me what I could become. I did not have anyone pushing me to do anything different than my parents or my family had already done. Instead, I looked around at my life and decided I wanted something different for myself.

After high school, I had several odd jobs. I worked as a bartender and enrolled in a technical college. I thought I wanted to be an architect, but I burned out from those classes pretty quickly.

Then, I got a job at Jiffy Lube. Every day, cars would come in, we'd change their oil, and then they'd go out. More cars would come in the next day, and we'd do it all over again—honest, important work.

One day, I was working on a Porsche. I have always loved Porsches—I still do. At that time in my life, I had never touched a Porsche. Of course, I was under the car and couldn't even see it. But I was still touching it. I took out the oil filter and realized it was an official Porsche filter, not like the generic one that I was about to replace it with. I decided to take it home with me to have some part of the car that I wanted so badly.

Of course, I was an idiot and tried to wash out the oil to clean the filter, not knowing how oil works. So, the filter ended up in the trash. But after working on that Porsche, I looked around at what I was doing every day, all day, and realized I'd never own a Porsche if I kept doing what I was doing. I told myself: *If you want something different in your life, you have to do something different.*

That's when I decided to go to college. I wanted to do something different and be something different than my family. No one told me to do this, but I chose to do it myself, for myself. Once I made this choice, it led to another question: how was I going to pay for it? I decided on the military because of my family background.

When you enlist, the first step is to take this massive test called the "Armed Services Vocational Aptitude Battery," or ASVAB. This is like a complex personality text, so you can't study for it. You just take it. This test will tell you, essentially, what you are capable of and where you might find your best fit in the military. Your scores will tell you if you are a fit for infantry, for example, or more specialized roles like logistics or operations.

Something surprising happened to me after I took this test: I scored very high. My recruiter basically told me that I could have any job I wanted within the military. This was completely different than my educational experience up to that point in my life. I had always had teachers tell me I was smart if I would just apply myself, but I had no interest in being the smart kid (which led to my 2.0 GPA).

Now, I had a test telling me that, objectively, I could do whatever I wanted. This was a new feeling for me. I began to think I was smarter than I gave myself credit for. It was another validation of my decision to go to college and try to find a different path than my parents.

I decided to go into the Air Force Reserves, working as a Fuel's Specialist. I went to basic training in May of 2001 at a base in San Antonio, then had my specialized training in Wichita Falls, TX, immediately after. I returned to Minnesota in early September 2001 and started college the next week.

At no point in this process did I have any external validation or anyone telling me what to do. In fact, when I told my friends and family I was joining the military, they all laughed and assumed I was joking. No one said I had to go to college or join the military. There were no standards for me to base my life on.

Now, my kids see me and my wife as successful professionals, but they don't know what we went through to get here. We've set different standards for my kids than my parents did for me. All my parents wanted from me was not to get brought home by the cops. My wife's parents, despite having a similar blue-collar lifestyle as my own, were the complete opposite. There was no question that she was going to college. She was always at the top of her class. If I was the teacher's nightmare, she was the teacher's pet. But we both had that same internal motivation that drove us forward.

She was a champion gymnast in high school and college, ranking at the state and national levels. She was motivated by her parent's high standards for her. She pushed herself because she knew her parents expected more of her. Our relationship was a huge factor in getting my act in gear and Figuring It Out. I knew that if I couldn't keep up, she'd one day ask herself what she was doing with this loser and leave me behind.

My kids, and people in general, seem to view success as an elevator ride up to the top floor. The truth is: it's stairs all the way up. You have to touch each one along the way.

If you look for motivation outside yourself, you're always going to look for someone to tell you what to do. Eventually, this will turn into you seeking someone to tell you it's okay to fail. If it's internal, you don't need someone else to tell you.

I tell my kids, "If you fail when trying your hardest, I'll pick you up and help you get back on the right path. But if you fail while refusing to try your hardest, you are going to have to pick yourself up."

At some point, kids have to stop looking to their parents to approve the choices they want to make and start validating those choices for themselves. For me, this happened when I realized that the future I wanted for myself was very different from the life my parents lived. They both worked very hard, but they never got ahead. After the military, they bounced around many jobs to try to find something that worked for them. At the same time, they were struggling to catch up financially. Without realizing it, solely by choosing my own path and committing to it, that need for external validation vanished.

Whether you are relying on your own self-limiting mindset or someone else's, you always have to push yourself to do what you need to do. Motivation comes from within—being able and willing to challenge yourself.

To succeed at this first habit of perseverance, you must find your own motivation and not look to others. If you are basing your life on your parents or some other family member, ask yourself: *Is this really what I want? Or is there something else I want out of life?* If the answer is yes, figure out what that is and commit yourself to that.

The "How" of How to Figure It Out

What happens if you seek out that external validation to keep you going? My wife has a friend who posts a selfie every day on social media. She doesn't work out of the house, her husband travels frequently for work, and her kids are off at college. She needs someone to tell her she's beautiful each day, and she does not have anyone around her to do it. And she can't look in the mirror and do it herself.

Instead of finding meaning within, this woman looks elsewhere for that motivation and that validation. Her motivation is entirely external, wanting to get as many thumbs-ups or likes as she can for how she chooses to live her life. That way, she knows she's on the right path.

If her motivation is feeling beautiful, that's her "why." Her "how" is looking to social media for some kind of external validation.

I don't know if this makes her happy, but I cannot imagine it does. I'm completely the opposite. A social media "like" means nothing to me. But give me a challenge, push me some way, tell me I can't do something, and I'll do it. Not only will I do it, but I'll also step on you, walk over you, and spit on you while I do it. Question what I can accomplish at your own risk.

People are often looking for someone else to validate what they do. The world we live in today is driven by online responses and reactions. People take to social media to complain about how expensive it is to live or how the daily commute to work impacts the time we have to go to the gym or hang out with our friends.

They say these things on social media because they are looking to their personal, hand-crafted network of people to feel sympathy for them and give them words of encouragement or simply for validation. But what is this encouragement going to change, other than keeping them on the same path they are on? Instead, they have to ask: *Do I have a choice? How can I Figure It Out?*

Maybe instead of scrolling on social media in bed or binging the next episode of that show you're watching, see if you can live with less sleep and work out in the morning. Readjust your weekends to spend more time with your friends rather than demanding that the universe grant you an extra hour each night to hang out just a little bit longer.

The only choice is how to Figure It Out in the context of the situation. For me, I decided to go to college and then start a business. For others, it may be sticking at that mechanic job and working their way up to owning the shop. Or, if you are trying to run a marathon or lose weight, it may be to get to the gym every day, no matter how many people see what you're up to on social media and give you the thumbs up.

We can choose to stay in our circumstances or pull ourselves out of the situation and try for something better. We can Figure It Out. This is why we are so fascinated by stories about rags to riches. Those that start out with only rags have every reason to stay where they are. But those of us who choose a different path, a different "how," only achieve our dreams by sticking with it—not because anyone told us any different.

Accountability: Find Your "Who"

Only about 9 percent of Americans actually accomplish their New Year's resolutions. Research shows that almost a quarter of people quit them *in the first week*. Nearly half have quit by the end of January.[1]

What happens then? People make the same resolutions the next year. That's why they are always the same each year: lose weight, make more money. But we don't stick with them. Many times, that's because these resolutions are externally driven. We see someone on Instagram who's in better shape than we are, so we decide that's what we want. Or we see our neighbor get a new, nicer car and decide we have to make more money to have that, too.

But even when we are internally driven to achieve something, and we've figured out the best way to do that, we still fail. That's because we haven't built up the right

---

[1] https://fisher.osu.edu/blogs/leadreadtoday/why-most-new-years-resolutions-fail

community around us. When we slip, nobody notices, so it doesn't really matter.

You choose to lose weight, get a gym membership, and make a habit of going to work out once every other day. You stick with it for a while, but then life gets in the way because, of course, it does. Life throws a lot of curveballs your way.

But let's say you add one more element to this habit: you bring along a friend. Guess what happens, then? You are much, much more likely to stick with your decision to go to the gym. Just telling someone you have a goal and making a commitment to them to achieve it results in a 65 percent chance of achieving it—way more than the 9 percent of people who complete their New Year's resolution. If you make that commitment and regularly check in with someone about your progress, you increase your chances of success by 95 percent.[2]

This is the last step for this habit: finding your "who." You have the "why" and the "how," and now you just need to be held accountable for following through on your decision. The best way to do that is with an accountability partner. You now ask yourself: *Who can I lean on?*

This may seem like a small thing, but it can make a big difference. You can almost double your chances of success

---

[2] https://observer.com/2017/03/psychological-secrets-hack-better-life-habits-psychology-productivity/

by creating an accountability relationship. That's a huge opportunity.

However, the opposite is also true if you surround yourself with people who give you a structure of permission to give up or fail; you are far less likely to succeed. If I'm significantly overweight and I want to lose weight, I can set a goal for myself. I can make a plan to go to the gym and eat healthy. But if my spouse is also overweight and doesn't want to lose weight, I should not expect them to be a great accountability partner or provide encouragement when I most need it. It doesn't work that way. Even if they're the most supportive person in the world, their "why" and "how" are different from my own. I need to find someone else to lean on.

These people might even actively inhibit you and what you want to achieve to preserve their own sense of self. If you change, that could threaten how they see the world. You are essentially showing them something else is possible if they just work for it.

This "who" question was something I struggled with the most during my time fighting off the lawsuits. My wife was on board with my "why" but not always my "how." She thought there was a better way for us to live the life we wanted, with less stress.

Instead of finding a level of support elsewhere, I chose to rely only on myself. This was a bad idea. It made things really, really hard for me. I could only turn to myself when I needed support, and while you need to look inside for motivation, looking inside for encouragement and accountability gets exhausting very quickly. That's why even the best athletes have coaches, and the most successful business people have mentors or peer support groups. As the Bill Withers' lyric goes: "We all need somebody to lean on."

If you decide you are going to go to college, but no one in your family has gone down that path before, you are intentionally choosing to do something different than they did. That person in your family, be it your mom or dad or uncle, isn't going to be the person to help you along the way.

Once you know your motivation, you can create that support network that helps you achieve what you want and need to achieve it. You can believe in your objective and find the people to help you get there. You have to believe what you do and say. But remember, the motivation has to come from within, not from what you think you are supposed to do.

Chapter 3: Be Self-Aware

Takeaways:

- One of the hardest things to do is to admit weaknesses.

- Avoid situations where you won't succeed—if you can't, learn from those situations.

- Recognizing areas of growth allows you to grow and achieve greater things.

When I was in my late twenties, my career was going pretty well. Those around me began noticing my drive, determination, and desire to learn. At the time, I worked as a consultant within a national financial service company, helping their regional branches expand their sales. I would go into places, share ideas for how to run things better (based on their objectives and what I was learning in other branches), and then move on to the next location. I had a reputation across the company as a hard worker and as someone capable of doing more.

Then, a different company decided to consider me for the role of "General Agent." This is essentially the person who "owns" the local business of the branch of the national company. General Agents were the people I'd been working with the most as a consultant, so I was, at least at a high level, familiar with the role. I would have my own company and my own team of agents under me, but we would benefit from our association with the national brand. The company I'd affiliate with would subsidize some of the expenses, help me out with some advice on how to get things started, and I would deliver on sales goals.

During the initial interview process, this company flew me to New York a few times from Minnesota (where I was living and working). These interviews would go on for days. In the last one, after many trips and meetings, a senior executive said to me, "I think you are smart and capable, but you are not ready for this role."

She was the only person who didn't think I was ready, but truth be told, she was the one person I was warned about. She had a reputation for being mean and very difficult. Up to this point, everyone else thought I was up for the job, so, ultimately, despite her opinion, they gave me the General Agent contract. I ignored her statement, feeling very confident with myself that I could get the job done.

I was taking over an office that already had some staff in place. The previous General Agent had left in a somewhat messy way, so I had some cleaning up to do. But with almost everything else in place, it seemed like a great way to get started.

The day I officially took over, I was standing in the front of the office, in front of about ten people, feeling a bit overwhelmed. I was no longer the consultant who could come in, make observations, share some knowledge, and leave it to the group to implement until I returned. I was now the person everyone was looking to for support through the grueling process of building a small business, and I was only a few years out of college.

I started to think that I should have paid more attention to the one person who thought I wasn't up for the job. Maybe she was right. Maybe what I took as a personal attack on me wasn't personal at all. Maybe what she was trying to tell me was that, although I had good experience, the specific requirements of this role were very different than anything I had ever experienced. Could she have presented her thoughts in a different way? Sure. But then again, would I have believed her? My self-confidence was so high I didn't want to question myself.

The problem with people who don't have self-awareness is that they don't know it (naturally). At this point in my life, I was not self-aware enough to know my faults. It was too late by the time I realized what I had gotten into as a General Agent. I was now in charge of recruiting, compliance, hiring, firing, managing a profit and loss statement, and otherwise making all other small and large business decisions. I had done none of those things at this point in my career. I may have made recommendations on these things as a consultant, and I may have been able to speak about them in my interviews, but I had never been the one to actually make the decisions. I had been recruited for this role, and that recruiter believed I was qualified for the role, even though he had also never seen the difference between advising on something and actually doing it. I was quickly and painfully learning just how different these two were.

So, did I admit my shortcomings and seek out people that could help? No. I was too afraid people would think that I was not ready for this opportunity. So, I struggled for two-and-a-half years. I learned a lot but ultimately stepped down from the role. I was at a conference in Florida with company leadership when I told them my decision to leave. They were a bit surprised to hear this since, at this point, I was actually showing results at a level better than most of my counterparts across the country. Nonetheless, they accepted my resignation. This mutual agreement and understanding is something that I will forever be eternally grateful for.

Do I regret taking on the General Agent role before I was ready? Absolutely not. Sure, at the moment I realized I had to leave, my pride took a hit. It's hard not to let something like that affect you initially. But for me, I very quickly got past that feeling of failure, and instead, my choice became liberating. Clarity is hard to find in life and even harder when you are struggling each day with a job or a task. When that struggle disappeared, I was finally able to focus on what I really wanted to do next.

Because of this clarity, the successes I had later in life were directly related to the failure I had in that position. In fact, I don't even consider this time in my career a failure but instead as the greatest learning opportunity I have ever had in business. I learned what I was good at. I learned what I was not good at. I learned what risks lie ahead if I am not honest with myself, and I learned that self-confidence will never be a substitute for self-awareness.

The next habit of perseverance is to be self-aware. For many people, this is the hardest thing in the world. We refuse to admit to ourselves who we are and what our choices mean. It's easy to lie to others, but ultimately, you cannot lie to yourself.

I go to the gym every day and on many occasions I'll see people who sit on the exercise bike and don't even pedal. They can go home and tell their friends and family that they were at the gym for an hour. But if they look at themselves in the mirror and say they are on their way to making a difference in their life, that is a straight-up lie.

Lying to yourself only hurts you and limits what you can achieve. Don't do it. Instead, know yourself and what you are capable of. That way, you can push yourself to do more and do better. Like me in my twenties, maybe you aren't capable of running a business on your own. But if you admit that to yourself right now, you can get on a path to becoming that leader you want to be.

Push and Learn

How many times have you been "voluntold" to do something? I hate that word. This is what happens in a professional setting when someone "volunteers" for a task or a role but doesn't really have a choice. They are essentially told what to do.

I did not ask for the General Agent job. I was recruited into it. Yes, I had a choice, but I knew I had to take it because it would be a hit to my self-confidence if I didn't. In that sense, I didn't really have a choice at all, and the recruiter knew this. Only one person throughout the interview process thought I wouldn't make it. She didn't say why. She just said she knew. The people who were interviewing me needed someone to fill the role, and they convinced me I could do it. I didn't argue with them. Maybe if that one interviewer had said more about why I wasn't the right fit, the others in the interview process would have seen that, too.

I was put into a position where I could not perform on my own, given my experience up to that point. I could have easily blamed the company leadership for this, and I am sure I did at times. Ultimately, though, it was my choice and my actions that led to what I viewed as subpar results.

Often, the person being voluntold what to do doesn't meet expectations. How could they? They didn't sign up for the task, even if it seems like they did. Consider the choice of the engineer who took over full development responsibilities after my uncle left my company following the lawsuit filing. Up until that point, this engineer had been focused on the backend (the stuff you don't see), whereas my uncle was focused on the front end (the stuff you do see). In the blink of an eye, he went from being part of a lethal two-man team building a fantastic piece of technology to filling the shoes of a 30-year software vet working on something he wasn't familiar with. So, what could he do? Blame me for this situation? Quit? Sure, this might help him feel better in the short term, but that wouldn't help when the next curveball would come his way.

Instead, what he did was stick up for himself and approach the challenge differently. He made it known what he could do and what he needed help with. I could have recognized my weaknesses much sooner than I did in my General Agent role and asked for help. Again, the problem with people who aren't self-aware is that they don't know that they're not. I could have said, "There is a long list of things I have never done before, and I could use some guidance to ensure I make the most of the opportunity." If you are given a task you aren't comfortable with, consider what my engineer said: "I'll take on the front-end development, but I'm going to need some time to fully understand how this works. I know I can figure it out, but please be patient with me while I learn." What I learned about this engineer, due to his accepting the responsibility, was that he was ten times more capable than he let on. For me, my overconfidence got me in trouble. His problem was the exact opposite.

Of course, no matter how self-aware you are, you are going to get into situations beyond your comfort zone. There's no way around it. If you push back every time you are in a tricky situation, you're going to get stuck in a rut you can't climb out of. And you'll never learn anything. Those around you will also probably get annoyed with you for not stepping up to try new things and take on hard projects.

Being self-aware is a delicate balance of acknowledging your weaknesses while also taking responsibility for situations. If you are in a new situation, ask those questions again: *Did I ask for this? Do I have a choice? What's the best way to Figure It Out?*

In almost all cases, the best way to Figure It Out is to push yourself by learning and embracing the growth mindset discussed in Chapter 1. You didn't ask for the situation, you didn't ask to be voluntold, but you were. Maybe you want to push back and get a better situation, but for whatever reason, you can't. Maybe it's because the coach just told you to play a new position, and the game starts in a minute. Maybe it's because your company has one last shot to launch a product, and they need everyone to do all they can to make it a success. Or, maybe it's because your company experienced some unexpected turnover, but the work still needs to be done. Sometimes, the only choice is for you to step up and go forward.

Who knows? Maybe you'll learn something about yourself you didn't know, and you'll find a whole new skill set you didn't know you had.

Take me as an example: When I was served my lawsuits, I made a choice to study the law like my business depended on it because it did. I had three lawsuits, so I became an expert on three substantially different subjects.

I was not going to allow myself to be surprised, so I had to be prepared.

That's Me, Knowing Me

The people who sued me thought I was going to be scared off by their legal action. But they clearly didn't know me because their action had the exact opposite effect. I wasn't scared, I was motivated. I knew myself, and I knew what motivated me. When I get pushed, I push back.

This is how I've always been, probably because of my military-brat upbringing. Living in over ten different cities and three different countries by the time I was in high school, dealing with the challenges of frequent uprooting, forced me to push myself. It was either driving myself forward or getting left behind. And I wasn't going to get left behind.

That's me, knowing me. As I said in the previous chapter, my wife had little interest in me fighting these lawsuits. She thought there was a better way for me to support our family than fighting for a business, which, at the time, had just started to get traction and was still a long way off from generating income for us.

When I was served those lawsuits, I was self-aware enough to know I wasn't going to quit. But unfortunately, I was not self-aware enough to see my weaknesses for what they were.

Being self-aware usually means finding something you might not like. We like to think about self-awareness as finding and growing our strengths, but it's also about acknowledging our weaknesses. That's much harder to do.

As I said, when you push me, I push back. This is not always the best course of action. Sometimes, a great strength in one situation is a disastrous weakness in another.

The reality of this is something that has taken a long time for me to recognize *and* be comfortable discussing. I'll be in a situation where I get jacked up about something, and it's not helpful. I am working on finding ways to help myself get brought back down when I need to.

I'll share my current relationship with my kids. They are both getting older and doing what young teens do: testing the limits of what they can get away with. I work extremely hard to get them to take responsibility for things like their homework, building friendships, and even their extracurricular activities.

Both of my kids are tremendously talented in their own way. My wife and I were athletes when we were younger, and at least one of us was a good student in school (as you can guess, that good student wasn't me). Both our kids inherited good genes. For my son, sports are his passion. Although quite athletic, my daughter's passions seems to evolve overtime and each year, seem to be more academic in nature. For her, and for most people who haven't fully committed to something, self-awareness can be even more elusive because it's hard to know when the passion for something is gone, or the challenge to push yourself is something you're unwilling to accept. For now, although she hasn't fully committed to something outside of academics, I love the fact that she's still exploring.

My son's passion is basketball, and his desire to be great has led him down a challenging path. When he was very young, his raw talent was enough to catapult him ahead of his peers in almost every sport he played. Now, as a high schooler, his raw talent alone could never be enough. Each year that has gone by, he has learned, by choice or by circumstance, to embrace hard work. With constant reminders from his parents and his coaches, he is grasping the reality that trying and failing creates some of the greatest teaching moments, no matter how hard it may be to see it at the time.

For both of my children, I struggle with their excuses for why they sometimes do not want to work hard through the challenges that come with learning. I find my energy level spikes whenever I feel like my kids are complaining or relying on excuses. I don't expect or demand that either of them get straight As or be the best in extracurricular activities, but I do demand that they be honest and don't use excuses. As I've said already, "Excuses don't solve problems." The lesson my kids learn each and every day is that you either raise your work ethic or lower your expectations. Of course, they are still kids, and I, too, must adjust my expectations of them from time to time.

Ultimately, I can't control what my kids do. I can only influence them. But I can control how I Figure It Out. This takes a level of self-awareness and self-confidence that some people, including me, at times don't have. And that can hurt.

When I failed as the General Agent, I could have given excuses, saying that it was a bullshit job at a bullshit company. Instead, I admitted I was not prepared for that role. I had that self-awareness, as painful as it may have been at the time to admit.

In other areas of my life, like with my kids, I found that self-awareness too late. I've come to realize that a lot of the tension in my life has come from my tendency to get overly frustrated. Especially when I'm pushed or when someone does not want to take responsibility for their actions. This is a good tendency, a good motivation. But I also can react too strongly, in a way that's over the top.

I am learning how to recognize this tendency within myself to harness the motivation differently and build myself up in a better way. If I'm getting to a point where I feel like a conversation with someone is going nowhere, and it's like we are looking at the same picture but see completely different colors—I see black, and they see red—then I need to move on. They probably aren't going to change their perspective. I need to try something different. Growing more frustrated never helps.

I've had discussions with a coach to find ways to better manage my tendency to respond to situations in too strong of a way. I go on an emotional roller coaster, with big ups and downs, rather than staying leveled out. I am working on recognizing when I get too jacked up and how to bring myself down from that. Sometimes, it's too late in a situation, but that's why I've acknowledged the problem, and I'm practicing something different.

Once, a customer of mine was six months behind on paying their bill. I kept reminding them, and they said they wanted a piece of information about their account before they paid. I told them where to find it and even did a screen share session. It was something easily accessible if they knew where to look. After doing this, I simply waited for them to get current on their bill.

Nothing. I reminded them again, and I got back an email from a senior executive, asking again for the information I had just told them how to find. She blamed me for the delay since I hadn't given them the information they wanted. As I had communicated, information like this was readily available to every customer, so there was no need to demand it from me. These delays had gone on for more than six months.

What should I have done? Just sent them the information in the email and called it done. They were too stubborn to find it themselves, but hey, dealing with stubborn people is the cost of doing business.

What did I do? I responded to the note in a very aggressive way, threatening to fire them as customers. I went way too hard, way too quickly. I made myself the jerk.

What ended up happening? I had to apologize, even though I felt I was right. I had to repair the relationship, and I ended up directly sending them the information they asked for. I did what I should have done in the first place. Then they paid their bill.

Once I identified this tendency in myself, I began asking myself my essential question: *How can I best Figure It Out?* I determined I had this problem within myself, and I wanted to change it. I was not blaming my upbringing for this issue, or my parents, or things that happened in childhood. All of that most certainly influences who I am and how I behave. But excuses don't solve problems. I have to be honest with myself about who I am and make the necessary changes.

I continue to work on this. I am using the habit from the previous chapter to help me define my "why," "how," and "who": I'm working to be a better dad and husband through intentional self-reflection. I know that I can't go to my wife or even my friends on this issue every time. They are too close to me. They have their own opinions on what I should do—some of which are very helpful. But I have to know what I want to do for myself.

The key element for building this habit (of self-awareness) is recognizing your own weaknesses for what they are and choosing how to Figure It Out. Just like you can't rely on others to make your choices for you, you can't change because someone else tells you to. It doesn't matter how many times someone hears they have a drinking problem—they need to recognize this problem for themselves before they can change.

Having this foundation of self-awareness will help you with every other habit of perseverance on your way to success.

Chapter 4: See Things in Black and White

One day, David Goggins decided to walk into a recruiter's office and enlist as a Navy SEAL. He was told he was way too fat. He'd have to lose over one hundred pounds in three months just to meet the weight requirements.

Given everything he had been through, you might have expected him to have walked right back out that door and not return; he had every reason to give up. As a kid, Goggins had an abusive father, struggled to learn, developed a stutter, was threatened with racial taunts in his small-town Indiana community, and was eventually diagnosed with sickle cell. This guy had more roadblocks than most.

What did he do? He doubled down on his decision to become a Navy SEAL. He pushed himself, lost 106 pounds, and went off to training.[3] He was assigned to SEAL Team 5 but did not stop there. Eventually, he decided to go to Army Ranger School. He is the only person to have been a Paratrooper, a Navy SEAL, and an Army Ranger. But that wasn't enough either: He decided to become an ultramarathoner, running for 24 hours at a time and completing races of over 300 miles.

---

[3] https://www.youtube.com/watch?v=5tSTk1083VY

How'd he achieve all this? It started with one simple commitment: he was going to lose that weight. That choice set him up for everything else.

Now, not everyone is David Goggins. Not all of us can relate to that.

But the commitment he made is relatable. It's simple but not easy. He made a decision, committed to it, and moved forward.

Someone a little more relatable than Goggins is me. I'm not a former SEAL or an ultramarathon runner, but I did commit. After barely graduating high school and working at jobs I felt were not long-term, I decided to go to college, enlist in the military, and eventually start a business. Following this path was my commitment to myself—an intentional choice to Figure It Out and get what I wanted. Goggins made a commitment to himself. We both followed through on it.

Before I made the commitment to college, the Air Force, and my future, I was wallowing away in choices. Choices, not commitments. I was changing oil and serving drinks on a path to nothing. To get out of this path of mediocrity, I had to make a commitment that required one hundred percent from me, nothing less.

When you are sort of committed to something, you will face reasons each day to give up. If you want to lose weight but are only sort of committed and wake up with a bit of cold, you'll give yourself an out to not go to the gym. When you are fully committed, you'll go each and every day. This then becomes something that you just do.

Throughout my commitments to myself, there were a lot of days that were harder than others. Following through really sucked. I would stumble, get tired, and even get sick. In December of 2022, just a few months before my trial started, getting sick took an unexpected turn, leading to six days in the hospital with pneumonia. But I was committed to keep going, with or without the oxygen tanks in tow.

The next habit of perseverance is about making these commitments. I call it "see things in black and white" because you can't be kind of or sort of committed. You either are or you aren't. No in-between. Either you are going to lose that weight, or you aren't. You are going to grow that business, or you aren't. You are going to run that marathon, or you aren't. There's no gray.

As a company owner, I have met many people who are searching for a new position. When I ask them why they are exploring new opportunities, many say they are "always looking." They keep their resumé up to date and are always exploring what else is out there. Maybe they even like their job and their coworkers, but they constantly want to know what else might be out there.

The dating world is no different. Listen to a thirty-year-old single person talk about dating and relationships, and you will hear the same thing: a lack of commitment. They want to keep their options open in case something better comes their way. Believe it or not, more choices make commitment harder: people who could choose a potential partner from a group of over twenty people were much less satisfied than those who chose from a group of about six[4]. When there's an almost infinite selection of people from your region—or even around the country—on a dating app, that makes it much easier to keep looking for that "perfect" fish in the big, deep sea.

Playing the field, in business and in personal relationships, may sound like a great idea, but it also prevents you from fully committing to where you are or who you are. What stuns me the most is when someone who doesn't commit acts surprised when their current relationship, whether business or personal, doesn't work out.

We think the grass is greener on the other side, but the grass is greener where you water it. If you commit to your patch of grass and tend to it, it can grow and thrive.

The value of this level of commitment is that you take ownership of what you are doing. After the actor Matthew McConaughey lost fifty pounds for the movie Dallas Buyers Club, he went on Joe Rogan's podcast. Rogan

---

[4]

https://www.tandfonline.com/doi/full/10.1080/15213269.2015.1121827

asked him why he tortured himself by losing all this weight for the role.[5]

McConaughey's response? "I was not torturing myself…the hardest part was making the damn choice." He said that if he hadn't made the choice to lose the weight but still had to go through what he did, it would have been hell. But he had made the commitment to himself, so he owned and controlled it. Sure, it wasn't easy to drop that much weight, but he was committed, and he did it.

He was able to do what he did because there was no gray area. There was just one choice. It was black and white.

If you have your motivation and you are self-aware enough, the next habit you can take on is to fully commit to whatever you are doing. You have to be fully devoted in achieving whatever it is you want to achieve.

Quit Your Side Hustle

I met someone who had started a company to create a product for the automotive industry. He had spent his entire life in this industry and knew this was an essential product with a large customer base. He had worked on this product for ten years outside his full-time job. He called it his "side hustle."

---

[5] https://www.youtube.com/watch?v=npJVN5-ZO2w

When I met him, I assumed his sales were through the roof, that he was having so much success that he didn't know what else was possible. But after ten years of hustling when he could, his sales were still terrible. Not much different than where he was when he started, even though the product had greatly improved. He knew that he should have been able to do better.

While speaking to him about it, I learned that he had outsourced his sales process to a third-party vendor. The thing was, this vendor had not made a single sale. Any sales he got came from him. Unfortunately, he was not good at marketing and had no idea who to call or contact to get the word out about his product. So, he landed a sale when he could, given his other responsibilities, and hoped the vendor would do more.

This guy believed he had a million-dollar product. He had convinced his wife that they could eventually retire on this idea. When I met him, he still believed it, even though he'd worked on it for years with no success. He had the conviction but not the commitment. He never fully committed to the product or himself, outsourcing to a vendor that couldn't deliver and giving the product the time he could when he could find it.

About 40 percent of those working full-time are like this guy and have a side hustle—some kind of business, product, or way to make money outside their full-time job. For millennials and Gen Z, this number is more like half. On average, these side hustles make people about $800 a month.[6] It's a pretty nice amount, but nothing that will dramatically change someone's standard of living.

What if these people had instead fully committed to their side hustle and saw what happened? Maybe they do all have million-dollar ideas, and that $800 could turn into $1,000, and then $10,000, and then who knows? These people won't because they won't jump all in and make that commitment to themselves.

What happens is that people get caught up in the beta test. They want to experiment with something and see what happens. They do their first experiment, maybe sell a little bit, but then things get hard, and instead of doubling down, they find another experiment to do. Or life gets in the way, and they can't find the time to give the idea or product the time it needs. They get caught in the "I'm going to see if this works" phase and can't get past it.

If you are stuck in this gray area, you are always going to look for excuses. You are always going to look for a reason why it doesn't work for you. Like the person relying on external validation, you are going to seek out something that validates what you think. That validates your opinions.

An honest, sustainable commitment takes time and preparation. When I made the commitment to start my company, I did not jump in headfirst. I had a full-time position somewhere else. I spent evenings and weekends

---

[6] https://www.bankrate.com/personal-finance/side-hustle-survey/

designing the product with my uncle, talking to people, getting their feedback, and putting the necessary legal documents in place. Essentially, in the eight months I was doing this research, I was also laying the foundation for my commitment.

At no point did I consider this business my "side hustle." I never saw it as a source for a far-off, future retirement. I saw it as a potential viable opportunity to provide for my family. Once the foundation was laid, I knew I was not going to turn back. I left my job and gave everything to the company.

In the Introduction, I shared the story of my friend who started an insurance business but quit after a few months. She never fully committed to it. When things got hard, she looked for people to validate her excuses: the economy was tough; no one returned her calls; the insurance provider was no help. Maybe that was all true, but she was telling herself these things so she didn't have to do the hard work that comes with commitment.

How long do you think she prepared before she jumped into the business? Probably not that much. Otherwise, she would have known about these challenges. She could have been having conversations to collect research, figuring out the roadblocks she'd encounter along the way. In the introduction, I talked about the growth mindset, in which you commit to learning more about what you can and can't do. But it's not enough to think you can do something. You must have the mental fortitude to handle the curveballs thrown your way. You have to understand how to Figure It Out.

There is a difference between laying the foundation for a future commitment and jumping in without knowing what you are doing. Often, jumping in too soon is a sign of a lack of commitment, not the other way around. If you want to ski black diamonds and do it well, you don't start at the top of the mountain. You start on the bunny hill.

You can't learn how to swim until you put your face in the water, blow bubbles, and overcome your fear of drowning. When you have both the conviction and the confidence in your decision, you'll know it's time to make a commitment. Once I had the foundation laid properly for my company, I committed. If I failed, I would fail by giving it everything. If I succeeded, I would succeed by giving it everything. Again, like I tell my kids, unless you are willing to give something your entire commitment, lower your expectations for what you are going to get out of it.

The choice to change or achieve something great is our own. And it's never too late to make a change. You aren't what you've done. You are what you repeatedly do.

If you choose to post pictures of yourself on social media repeatedly, that's who you are. You are the person who seeks external validation to feel good about yourself. You need those likes and comments, and each day you do it, the harder it is to break that habit the next day. If you keep tinkering away at your side hustle without actually putting in the work, your side hustle will always stay on the side. If you continue to go to the one friend who always agrees with your reason not to do something, then you are someone who relies on excuses rather than solving problems.

But even if you have repeatedly chosen to live this way for your whole life, there's good news: that's all in your past. That's what you did. Now, you can make a different choice for what you want to do repeatedly. You can know yourself better, make a commitment, and act on that.

Instead, we rely on the past to define our future. People don't create the future with the future; they create it with their past. All doubts and failures, for many, dictate the future; however, they do not accurately reflect what can be accomplished or what can be achieved.

"Comparison is the thief of joy." That quote is attributed to Theodore Roosevelt and many, many others because it's a good saying. If we spend our time worrying about what others think, what others have accomplished, and what others are doing rather than what we want, we are never going to be able to get to where we want to be.

If you repeatedly compare yourself to others, you are never going to figure out who you actually are. Looking for those "likes" on Facebook is really about living in a safe, controlled environment where validation comes easily. Instead, we need to get outside our comfort zone—the trap of our past and what we think others are doing—and push ourselves to do more.

I've been to Disney World many times. Too many times. I hate it. But my kids and in-laws love it. Unfortunately, the dad does not always get to choose the vacation.

In my experience, Disney is 95 percent frustrated parents with their kids, and 5 percent smiling at the camera. When everyone comes back from the trip, guess what they show people? The smiling pictures. Guess what they post on social media? The one picture from the one moment where everyone wasn't getting on each other's nerves. They leave out the agony of the long lines on the crazy hot days when kids won't stop complaining or the shot of expensive food that no one ate. Everyone says, "Oh, what a fun trip you had!" and wishes they could do the same. It's all fake nonsense.

We have to move past the fake nonsense. We are stuck in what we repeatedly do rather than Figuring It Out to get to who we want to be. The best way to do that is to commit ourselves and, ideally, as I discussed in the last chapter, make that commitment to others as our accountability partners to help keep us on track.

When we do this, we'll wake up every day and do whatever we can to fulfill this commitment.

Chapter 5: Don't Take "No" for an Answer

Takeaways:

- A "no" isn't the end of the world. See it as a learning opportunity.

- Take things one step at a time to persevere through challenges.

- Keep your cool and have patience on your journey to success.

I shared the story in an earlier chapter about how one of my first sales calls for my new business was to the largest financial services company in the country. Well, I didn't stop there. I also reached out to the second-largest financial services company to see if they were interested.

I had a little more success with this company, let's call them Acme Financial Group. After the initial call, I had many conversations with them and presented our product several times. They were very clear with me about what they needed from us and what our product had to do if we wanted their business. Acme Financial Group provided fantastic feedback and suggestions that guided some of the decisions we made in the development of our product. I had developed a very close relationship with my contact there, and he had become a friend. I was confident we were going to land the deal.

After several months of back-and-forth, in 2018, I was in Disney World with my family. (They had forced me to go once again.) I got a call from my friend, and I stepped out of line for the ride we were waiting for to take it. I was thrilled to see his name on my phone, distracting me from the screams of children around me. The company had a contract in hand, and all I needed from them was a signature. I knew this call would be the moment we got the deal.

Instead, guess what he said? "Sorry, I've been overruled." Someone above him had made the decision that instead of going with my company, they had chosen a competitor. This other company was new to this technology like we were; however, the company itself had been around longer and was more well-known. What would have been our biggest deal at the time fell through in a matter of seconds.

I was beyond upset. I had spent so much time cultivating this potential client, and I felt so confident it would happen. But I didn't show that frustration. It was uncharacteristic of me, sure, but it helped that my friend was genuinely sorry and frustrated with me about this decision. There was nothing I could do. So, I thanked him for his time and support of what I was trying to do, hung up the phone call, and sat down on a bench as the Disney masses swarmed all around me.

I could not believe what I had just heard. I wasn't so arrogant that I had started to make business plans for the deal we did not yet have, but I had mentally accepted that this client was coming my way. I didn't know what we'd do now that it wasn't.

But there was one thing I did know: I was not going to take their "no" as the final answer. I saw this decision on their part not as a "never" but as a "not right now" or a "not yet." The way I thought about it, the other team—my competitor—had not won, but I had lost. I just needed to learn what I could do to make a better product, sell it better, or communicate better. I would get that "yes" eventually.

Don't get too freaked out by a "no." For so many people, hearing "no" is emotionally paralyzing. They don't know how to handle it. That kind of rejection crushes them, like how a scale that doesn't go down crushes someone trying to lose weight.

But a "no" is not the end of the world. There will always be other opportunities for you, and even things you thought weren't going to happen can come back around. You have to believe in yourself and keep going.

An important part of the Figure It Out mindset is not taking "no" for an answer. This requires professional perseverance. Success takes a long time—it's dirty and brutal. You are not getting atta-boys every day. If the last chapter was about staking your commitment to yourself, this chapter is about not losing sight of that commitment and how to keep up that focus and energy to get to where you need to be.

What does this professional perseverance look like? Respectful connections while offering value.

After I got that "no" from my friend at Acme Financial Group, I stayed in touch. I didn't badger, but I did not let the relationship die, either. I had gotten to know this guy, and I would check in from time to time. I knew about his family, so I asked about his kids when I thought they must be going off to college. I would give him updates on our product. I would share with him industry updates, like when a company got fined by a regulator, and told him I wanted to make sure his company wouldn't make the same mistake.

Did he respond to these emails? Not always. But I knew he got them, and he kept seeing my name. He knew that I was continuing to improve.

Now, there's a fine line between being persistent and being a pest. I hope my professional perseverance never crossed that line. But many people cross it: think of the real estate agent who hears you are interested in a house and then sends you automated updates on similar homes daily. There's no value there and no personal, professional connection.

I made sure that my outreach to my friend—or any of the dozens of other representatives at companies I stayed in touch with—never seemed canned or superficial. I didn't do the thing where I sent an email every first of the month or on their birthday. They'd see through that too quickly. Sometimes, I'd send the email on a weekend because maybe they happened to be looking at their inbox at that time. Who knows?

Two years later, after many of these touchpoints with my friend, I got another call from Acme. They wanted to fly me out and talk more about my product. Apparently, it wasn't going well with my competitor. I got this call right around the time I was served my lawsuits in early 2020, so it wasn't great timing. But of course, I took that flight to their headquarters in California. I made it happen.

I got there, pitch-ready, but here's what they told me: they were switching to me. After being strung out for months, confident the deal was mine, then blindsided with a straight "no," I had finally gotten the "yes." It didn't come how I wanted or expected, but it came.

I didn't take "no" for an answer. And I figured out my way to the sale.

One Step at a Time

Do you want to hear something crazy? Every single company that told me "no," every single one became customers and clients. This wasn't just one or two companies. This was dozens of firms.

How did I develop a product that ended up kicking the shit out of my competition? I didn't let the tail wag the dog. No one understands what a financial advisor does better than a financial advisor. No one understands what a compliance officer needs better than a compliance officer. I had been both. No other company was building a product with the end user in mind. I was. They were all thinking about the person signing the contract, whereas I was thinking about how to create the most value for the people who were going to be using my product. You may be surprised to hear that companies build their products without considering the customer. But I can assure you, sit in enough engineering meetings, and you will see firsthand how infrequently the customer comes up in conversation.

Remember the Segway? It was hyped as a revolutionary personal transportation device when it was launched in the early 2000s. But it never lived up to its expectations because it was built to solve a problem that didn't exist: the need for a new form of personal transportation. So many companies decide to make products without considering what a customer would actually think about it once they have it in their hands.

My competitors all had engineers designing their products. But I had someone designing ours—me—who knew exactly what was needed in a product like this. We didn't have the best product right away, but with every "no" that I received, I learned from the experience, which made what we were offering even better.

The person who improves over time to get good at sales is the person who doesn't fear the "no." For me, every "no" was one step closer to a "yes." For some, every "no" makes the phone weigh ten pounds more than it did before the last call. After a few "no's," the phone weighs too much even to pick up.

I get it. No one wants to hear a "no." When I got that call at Disney World and learned I was not getting that huge contract I assumed was mine, I was crushed. But it happens. You can't dwell on it. You must pick yourself up and move on.

But easier said than done, right? Each "no," day after day, can feel like a kick in the crotch. Why put yourself through all the pain?

You'll often hear people talk about "two steps forward and one step back." You make it to one goal but then fail in some way that makes it seem like achieving your goal is a bit harder than before. You can still see the end in sight, but it's not as close as you hoped.

That's all BS. Talking about going two steps forward and then sliding back a bit makes it seem like failure pushes you backward. It's not. Each rejection is actually a step forward towards where you need to go if you learn from it. It may suck in the moment, but rejection isn't always bad.

You don't have to see rejection as something all-encompassing, something connected to who you are. Instead, see it as one step of many on your path to success.

You have to take small steps to go a long distance. It's impossible if you try to take on the long-distance all at once. But one milestone at a time, one objective at a time, makes it easier. How many steps back would you consider one major lawsuit? How about three?

Think of a sales call not as a make-or-break situation but as a way to learn more about what the customer wants. That's how I approached it with my sales. I spent months learning about what my potential customers needed. Sure, I was upset when they didn't go with me, but it helped me improve my future sales. I was able to learn more and more with each step along the way, bringing me closer to my ultimate goal of developing a successful, sought-after product.

I also learned different approaches to the act of selling. I began my pitches with the compliance officers at the financial services companies but quickly realized that they were not the final decision-makers on whether or not I'd get the sale. They also weren't going to see the potential of my text-to-client product since they didn't interact with clients. I had to work through the financial advisors instead, who knew how much easier their lives would be with what I was selling.

If I had seen the rejection I received as some kind of final statement on my worth or my company's worth, I'd have given up right away. Instead, I saw them as a learning opportunity to improve what I was offering. This is why I could turn those first "no's" into final "yes's."

A "one step at a time" mentality helps you redefine success on your path to your goals. Instead of working for weeks towards a big sale or product launch, you can find success in a cold call that went well or a team meeting that generated a lot of good ideas. You build from these small steps towards your bigger picture.

This approach is not only for professional perseverance, either. It's just as appropriate to overcome personal struggles. Andy Stumpf, a retired Navy SEAL and podcast host, talked about how going through a divorce was the most challenging time in his life. Harder than anything in his military career. He said it was the lowest point for his self-worth. He questioned everything about himself.

Stumpf could have seen this personal struggle as many steps backward—maybe all the way back to the beginning—but he didn't. He was able to reflect and see the beauty in his pain. He knew there was an opportunity for self-reflection and growth.

But it was still hard, of course. How'd he make it through? He broke his goals down into "super small, digestible chunks."[7] During his military training, that would be to make it to the next week or the next session. Throughout his divorce, some days, his goal was to make it through a Zoom call or see the sun the next day.

Not taking no for an answer starts with being honest with yourself. If you can't be honest with yourself, you will learn nothing. That commitment to learning will help you move from the "no's" to the "yes's." I fought hard with my business to find out why someone gave me the "no," regardless of what I'd learn. Believe it or not, I didn't always agree with the answer I received, but that wasn't

---

[7] https://www.youtube.com/shorts/MFA05xgglOE

my decision. Once I understood the reason for the no, I could then focus on what to do to prevent another no for the same reason.

The same goes for your personal life. You may not fully own every problem within any relationship, but don't be so self-centered as to think you don't own at least some of it. Maybe you weren't the one who started the fight this time, but if the same fight keeps happening again and again, you have to be honest with yourself that you are bringing something to the problem.

In business, marriage, heck, life, it's amazing how much we can lose when we focus on being right.

Do whatever you need to do to get through life's crush. Make it work for you. Whether that's pass after pass of potential customers or the weight of breaking up a family, you can get through it if you just don't take "no" for an answer.

Keep Your Cool

I'll admit I'm not the most patient guy. This is especially true with my kids. I'll tell them to do something, and they just don't listen. Like I said in the last chapter, I see things in black and white. If I tell my kids to go to bed, they should go to bed. If they are hungry, they should sit down and eat their dinner. The best way I know for someone to stop being hungry is to put food in their belly.

But my kids don't always see it this way. They'll stare at their plate for ten minutes, complaining that they want something else to eat. Or I have to tell them six different ways that it's bedtime. Or if my son is doing his weekly chore of cleaning up outside, he comes back inside when half the yard is still covered in dog poop.

I can get frustrated. I don't want to sit and hold their hand throughout all of this. I have an expectation of how long something should take, and my kids have different expectations.

Unfortunately, with professional perseverance, there are going to be different expectations. You are going to expect something at a certain time or in a certain way, and that won't happen. It might take two years and maybe a few failed engagements with your competitors until that client comes back your way.

This is why learning to deal with rejection—to not take "no" for an answer—isn't just advice for people in sales. I've been told I'm good at sales, but I've never considered myself a salesperson. I just think of myself as good with people and understanding of whatever comes my way. This helps me be good at professional perseverance. I don't take things personally, and I proceed by learning about what I can do better.

If you go out for a promotion and don't get it, that "no" can be seen as a rejection, or it can be seen as a "not yet." You can learn and grow and make yourself a better candidate for next time. Sure, losing out on a promotion can be seen as going backward, but maybe if you did get that job, you would quickly be in over your head. Instead, focus on learning what you need to learn to be a better candidate for the promotion and to perform at a higher level.

Don't lose your cool when you don't take "no" for an answer. Have patience with your perseverance. If I had exploded on the phone with my friend from Acme Financial Group when he called me at Disney World, there would be no way I would have gotten that deal two years later.

I just stayed the course like nothing had changed. I was that duck on the pond, paddling furiously, but all anyone saw was me calmly floating across the water. And anyway, I had so much else to do! I spent a lot of time getting more users, building my team, and, of course, fighting the lawsuits when those came to my door—but I also had to keep in touch with everyone else who had told me "no." Devoting mental energy to all those follow-ups and touching base with everything going on? It became a habit. It was simple but not easy. But it was important and needed to be done.

Sometimes, that's hard, but you have to do it if you want to come out on the other side successful.

The End of the World

If you remember, the second and third lawsuits were served to me in March of 2020, just a week or so before the world shut down during the Covid lockdown. I thought the lawsuits were as bad as it would get, but a global pandemic was right around the corner. If I wanted to find an excuse to give up, there were a lot for me to choose from.

But I also got the call from Acme Financial Group to come back to pitch again at the same time. I had no choice but to fly to their headquarters in California while figuring out what to do about the lawsuits. Rumors were flying around about what would happen with Covid. Europe was shutting down, and I didn't know if I'd make it home from California.

This company first went with my competitor in March 2018. I got my "yes" on March 12, 2020.

That night, I went to a bar to celebrate. I was watching the news, where they were discussing the decision for the NHL to suspend their season. This came a day after the NBA had suspended their season.

A "no" isn't the end of the world, but on that day, it sure seemed like the world was ending. There were a lot of challenges to come for me personally (and the rest of the world), but on that night in the bar, the beer went down smoothly, and the burger was delicious. I had persevered and gotten the "yes."

I hope that we never go back to that place in March 2020. But even though things were bad, I was still able to push through the pile of muck that was the world back then and grab on to a win. No matter what muck you are wading through in your life, you can always find some way to get that win, no matter how small.

Chapter 6: Redefine Your Goal

Takeaways:

- A goal is an input, not the outcome.

- Success cannot be treated as a light switch.

- Align your goals with the state of success you want to achieve.

The wife of a friend of mine wanted to lose weight. She did what many people do: she set a goal for herself (losing forty pounds) and then made a plan to reach that goal. She ordered a lot of fancy foods and supplements to help her eat healthy and lose that weight.

And she did it. After a few months of eating this expensive food, she hit her target. She was thrilled, of course. She had worked hard and achieved her goal. She got herself a new wardrobe to celebrate and got rid of all her old clothes. She turned the page and was ready for the next chapter.

I imagine you or someone you know can relate to this. We've all been there, working hard towards some kind of personal goal about our bodies, either trying to lose weight, get in some kind of shape, or look a certain way.

You achieve your goal, but then what happens? Well, my friend's wife stopped buying those fancy foods and went back to her old diet, slowly, over time. As she did this, her weight crept back up. After a few more months of her old lifestyle, she was at her old weight. But this time, she was stuck with a bunch of clothes that didn't fit her.

The weight loss industry is valued at about $225 billion and is expected to grow to over $400 billion by 2030.[8] That's a lot of money for something we already have the answer to and have had the answer to for about as long as there have been humans: eat right and exercise.

That's the secret to losing weight and keeping it off. Eat the right amount of food for your body and do enough exercise to burn excess calories. Nothing more, nothing less. The hardest part is not in the losing but in keeping it off.

The weight loss industry makes a fortune by convincing people that it can make them skinny again, while pharmaceutical companies make a fortune by helping overweight and unhealthy people to live with their decisions. People are looking for answers outside of themselves rather than doing the simple but hard work of Figuring It Out on their own.

What do we get from this? Nearly one in three adults in the United States are overweight, and two in five are

---

[8] https://www.fnfresearch.com/weight-loss-and-weight-management-market

obese.[9] The weight loss industry and the pharmaceutical companies are pulling two different ends of the same rope, and neither side actually cares about the outcome because that pull and push is how they make money.

The weight loss industry wants to sell you easy fixes and schemes to think you can get around the hard work it takes to do this. But it won't work. You'll never keep off the weight if you go back to your old ways. The longer you ignore this, the harder it becomes to get back to where you belong.

You can set a goal to lose five pounds, ten, or one hundred. You hit that goal, but then you slip back into old habits. You achieved your goal, so why keep up that intense exercise routine or keep paying for all those supplements? You don't think you need to anymore, and you are probably exhausted from putting in all the energy it takes to stick to your commitment. That's why anywhere from 80 to 95 percent of dieters gain back the weight they lost.[10] They focus their goal on the end result only, not the habits along the way.

---

[9] https://www.niddk.nih.gov/health-information/health-statistics/overweight-obesity
[10] https://health.clevelandclinic.org/why-people-diet-lose-weight-and-gain-it-all-back

If your goal is to lose thirty pounds, you will only work hard enough to lose thirty pounds. Once you reach it, that work is done.

That's why you need to change the goal from the ultimate outcome you want to achieve to one of your inputs to eventual success.

What do I mean by this? Consider the context of losing weight. If your goal is to lose twenty pounds, that's a starting point. Then, you figure out the eating habits you need to lose that weight. Your goal then becomes maintaining the habits rather than some arbitrary number to lose.

For me, I try not to eat anything until lunchtime. This allows my body to leverage something called ketosis. Another thing I did years ago was sign up for a food tracking app, which told me how many "points" I could have each day. Each item I ate or drank reduced my available remaining points. There was a sandwich place near my office where I loved to eat. But the problem was this one sandwich consumed 100 percent of my daily points. Thanks to the insight I got from the app, I quickly stopped eating there.

Or consider how most sales companies focus on the number of phone calls made to prospective customers, frequently referred to as "dials." The thinking goes, the more dials you make, the more sales you make. But that's completely backward: you can crush your dials all day long but not make a single sale if you only care about getting to the next call. When I worked at a call center, I changed the goal, so it wasn't the dials but having meaningful conversations. The best sales reps had lower dials but longer call times. We created a habit of connecting with prospective clients and customers, which helped us achieve the ultimate outcome of running a successful sales company.

Your Goals Run You

Goals have a tendency to take over your life. You want to lose a certain amount of weight or make a certain amount of money. Much of this turns into a kind of "keeping up with the Joneses" desire to achieve the external validation I discussed in Chapter 2.

You may have a friend or neighbor who exudes success: fancy cars, clothes, or a giant house. But you don't know if they are one paycheck away from bankruptcy. Believe it or not, a 2023 survey found that 78 percent of Americans live paycheck to paycheck.[11] They may be afraid to give up the aesthetics of their life, so they keep on spinning in a job that gives them the money they need for a lifestyle that doesn't particularly make them happy. And then you are afraid of what it means that you do not have the "success" this other person seems to have.

---

[11] https://www.forbes.com/advisor/banking/living-paycheck-to-paycheck-statistics-2024

If your goal is to have the nicest truck, you may find yourself working towards this goal. When you've got the nicest truck on the block, then what? Get an even nicer truck? Move on to the best TV? You'll always find something else to buy.

I don't care about getting the best or newest stuff because I don't care what anyone thinks of me. I have what I consider a nice truck, but if I started comparing myself to everyone else around me, that opinion might change quickly. Remember, "Comparison is the thief of joy."

When setting a goal for yourself, think about what you want your life to look like. Think about what your day-to-day is. Your goals shouldn't run your life. Instead, they should be a part of your life. See them as incremental steps along the way toward success.

When I worked as a financial advisor, many people came to me and asked if they could retire. My answer was always "yes." They were happy to hear this, but then I added the important caveat: "but let's talk about your spending habits first." Anyone can retire, but it depends on how much they want to spend when they retire. They must have spending habits that fit their finances.

Instead of caring what the neighbors think and spending to keep up with them, focus on what you want out of your lifestyle—such as retiring, maybe—and then work to fit your life to what you want it to be. Not what you think someone else wants it to be.

I know an incredibly intelligent and beautiful woman…okay, it's my wife. At one point in her career, she found herself coveting a certain title: director. I don't think she could even say why, but it probably had to do with her peers and friends with similar work experience reaching these higher leadership positions in their own companies. She wanted this title and all the responsibilities and expectations that came with it.

When this goal crept up, she had a great role and was very good at it. She received high praise and annual pay raises with good bonuses. But this wasn't enough. She wanted that title. She interviewed for a role at a new company and received the offer she wanted because she is very talented. Prior to accepting it, she and I discussed what she was walking away from and what she was walking into. She knew she had a great position in a great company with a team she liked, but she really wanted this, so she took the job. I supported her, of course. It was what she said she wanted. We both thought she would love it, and we celebrated her success and achievement of the stated goal.

I'll bet you can guess what happened: she was miserable. The company she left was filled with supportive coworkers and leaders. What she found in this new role was significant animosity, more tension, and a constant lack of support from leadership. Every day, she felt like she was set up to fail, and there was a growing line of people waiting for that to happen so they could take over her position.

We learned an important lesson from this experience: be careful what you ask for because you just might get it.

A goal isn't a bad thing, inherently. But it shouldn't be the end result. It should be an input into what you want to achieve. Let's say my wife wanted the title to receive some kind of recognition for her work or to feel valued or appreciated. Her goal—the title—should have been an input into her broader definition of success that also included more holistic definitions, including being able to spend time with family.

Over the years, I've been invited to college campuses to talk to business students about how to be a successful business owner. I typically start off my talks by asking them: "If you run your own business, how many hours a week do you work?"

They'll answer forty, fifty, sixty. I'll just stare at them.

I give them a few tries and then share the real answer: "All of them."

At these schools, business students and entrepreneurship majors are told all the cool things that come with running a business. The freedom, the chance to build something for yourself, even the fancy titles you get on your social profiles, like CEO or President. It's a shot at making it big. But they don't talk about the stress and how running a business takes you away from other things you want in life.

Your ability to achieve something is based on what you are willing to give up. When I was fighting my lawsuits, I gave up sleep. That maybe wasn't the best decision for my health, but it helped me learn what I needed to learn to fight back.

Or consider a sports analogy. How many examples are there of a hotshot athlete drafted as the "next big thing" only to end up as a bust as a professional? This could happen for many reasons, but one of them could be that the athlete has the draft as an end goal rather than an incremental one along the way.

One athlete who sacrificed almost everything for his sport was Chad Ochocinco. Once he was drafted by the Cincinnati Bengals, the NFL wide receiver decided to actually live at the stadium for two years. He was completely focused on his game and improving. He didn't need anything else.[12]

Ochocinco could have gotten drafted, made it to the big leagues, and coasted on his initial success. Instead, after being drafted, he knew the real work had begun. Being drafted was not the goal but simply a milestone along the way. He couldn't relax, stop grinding, or work to get better. In fact, he understood that he had to work harder and smarter than he ever had.

---

[12] https://people.com/sports/chad-ochocinco-johnson-says-he-lived-inside-the-cincinnati-bengals-stadium-for-two-years

This is just as true for being an entrepreneur. If you want to make a lot of money, there are many ways other than running your own business. If you want freedom, there are other ways you can get it. You have to figure out exactly what you want and why and then figure out all the different inputs into that definition of success. Otherwise, you are going to be stuck in a situation you do not want.

This is the ugly part of being an entrepreneur that is seldom taught and often ignored.

The Motivation Industry

I have a home gym, but I never use it. I walk by it every day on my way out the door to my other gym.

I know myself, as I talked about in Chapter 3. I know that if I'm going to work out, I need to be around other people. That's what energizes me.

Being honest with yourself about what motivates or energizes you is half the battle. People love telling lies to others to make themselves feel better, but the lies they tell themselves cause the most damage.

I know for a fact that I need to go to a gym with other people to get in the right mindset to exercise. I don't know why, but a home gym is too easy to walk past and say, "I'll do it later." Later today becomes tomorrow, tomorrow becomes next week, and next week is never.

Instead of a weight loss industry, we need a motivation industry. We need to help people find their path to motivation and stick to it. Setting smarter goals allows us to find motivation, create habits, and have small, sustainable wins along the way.

If you want to get out of bed and get to work, you need to figure out: *what do you want, and why?* The first part of this question is pretty common, and you probably have an easy answer. The second part, though, is much more difficult. What you say may actually change your answer to the first part.

If you find yourself asking for something that requires external validation points, like "I want to make a lot of money so my family will be proud of me," then you will always struggle with motivation.

Having a goal like "losing weight" or "getting a new title" is answering the "what" but not the "why." It's replacing your state of success with some kind of tangible external factor that's easy to point to and say, "Yeah, that's what I want." If you want your family to be proud of you, do you think you need to make a lot of money? Or do you think you need to be a good spouse and parent? Determining what makes you a good spouse and parent is much harder than just getting a big paycheck each week.

Because success isn't about flipping a light switch; you aren't going to lose that weight or get that job, and then, boom, the lights are on, and you are happy and satisfied. Success takes hard work and perseverance. You need to stay motivated throughout. Building in those Figure It Out habits is the hardest thing to do.

Get Goal Alignment

Once you know what motivates you and you've got good habits for Figuring It Out, you also need to figure out how to align your goals with your ultimate vision for success.

Let's revisit my wife's corporate career. The director role she took, along with being extremely challenging, also proved to be extremely educational. As her career progressed, she was provided more opportunities to grow and climb the corporate ladder.

She eventually found her way to a great senior leadership role in a large organization, with a fantastic team and consistent opportunities to show her capabilities. As the role evolved, however, the demands began to change. This remote role with limited travel shifted quite rapidly to some and then suddenly, extensive travel. To some, eager to grow in their careers, this shift might be seen with excitement and enthusiasm; however, my wife does not get too excited about getting on a plane and certainly isn't thrilled about doing it as frequently as the company now expected.

For her, not seeing her family presented a significant challenge. Although her colleagues and superiors had families of their own, they didn't seem to mind missing time at home. The reality for her was she wasn't really interested in moving up any further in the corporate world. She no longer felt the need to continue pushing to show she was capable and willing to do more. In fact, the constant travel made it difficult to support her current team and workload.

The misalignment came when she finally approached her boss about the travel situation. As the company grew, the demands of her leadership role changed, and unfortunately, she was faced with a decision: embrace the change or leave the role.

So, she put in her notice and found something better. She finally decided to pursue her passion: interior design. She felt compelled to compete in the corporate rat race for the sake of a paycheck and a title. When she finally realized these two external motivators would not lead to happiness, she made the brave choice to do something she wanted to do, not what she thought she was supposed to do.

When I first sought out investors for my tech company, I started with my personal and professional network. Lucky for me, I didn't need to look any further. I secured three investors right away, but I needed one more to get the necessary funding.

I found someone from my network to fill this last slot, but this guy was super focused on his rate of return. The other three knew they were investing in me and also knew I need time to build a successful company. The fourth one would constantly hound me about what he could expect from his investment. I don't blame him, of course, as ROI is a critical goal for the investment, but at this early stage, that should not have been the singular focus.

I knew this particular investor would most likely cause frustration for me. I had no way of knowing what his ROI would be because I had no idea myself. I had no logical way of forecasting his return in a way that would ever satisfy him.

So, I chose to find another investor to round out the four I was seeking. I got someone who was much similar to the three I had—committed to me as a person and interested in a company's long-term growth beyond a set ROI. The initial three investors all received their initial investment back, with some interest, only a couple of years into this business venture. The last investor, the one added at the end, chose to stick it out for the entirety of the business process, including all the lawsuits, and as a result, received a significant return on their investment.

I had found investors aligned with what I was trying to do and the level of support I needed. This allowed me to build the business I desired to build and generate a significant return for everyone.

Success: The Last Thing You Do

When I was a financial advisor, most of my clients were fifty-five and over. I had the credentials to work with many individuals nearing retirement, each of whom was trying to understand how to retire effectively and—most importantly—do so comfortably.

When I met these people, I talked about their previous relationships with financial advisors and asked them if they ever discussed their goals. Not surprisingly, the answer was always yes. What surprised them was my response. No one expected someone like me, this financial advisor with a track record of success, to look them in the eye and tell them I don't care about their goals.

What would follow after I dropped that bomb was a series of questions so I could gauge how well they were doing, not just towards their goals, but as a whole, financially. It always amazed me to see smart people so focused on retirement or paying for their kids' college that they would completely ignore the importance of having a proper cash reserve. Or why a proper estate plan is imperative, or even how life insurance or the lack thereof can ruin everything if something unforeseen happens. My approach was fundamentals first and goals second.

After walking through these fundamentals, people got it. In fact, they loved it. I built a tremendous business that made other advisors scratch their heads because I wasn't following the standard playbook for financial advising. It wasn't because I could pick stocks better than they could; we all had the same information there. Instead, I helped people prioritize.

Imagine not starting with how much weight you want to lose but rather with the habits you need to create. Maybe it's carving off time in your schedule to exercise, not buying junk food so you're not tempted to have it around at home, or reducing the amount of alcohol you consume. What if, instead of the numbers on the scale, you measured progress based on how you're doing with the fundamentals you have determined are important to you, not anyone else?

Imagine not starting with the title or the salary you covet but rather with the habits you need to create to be sought after for a promotion so that the fight is no longer needed. Maybe you choose to begin reading leadership books and implementing the small things that catch your attention. Maybe you hire a business coach or mentor to help you understand how to be a more effective leader.

Once you have all these habits down to a point where it's not a struggle to do them every day, then, and only then, you can begin to consider what you want to achieve for your state of success.

The legendary wide receiver Jerry Rice said that the thing he focused on the most was his exercise routine.[13] Not catching practice, just the basics of exercise. He knew that if he did this every day, repeatedly, catching the football would be easy. It would just be the last thing he did.

Once you have your habits in place, whether that's exercise, eating right, reading leadership books, or whatever it might be, success is just the last thing you do.

---

[13] https://jamesclear.com/jerry-rice

Chapter 7: Be Humble

Takeaways:

- Confidence without humility is arrogance.

- Be a chameleon leader, not a seagull.

- Don't be the boss, be the example.

Once, very early on in my career, I was being interviewed for a management position. I was asked to share three adjectives that others I'd worked with might use to describe me. I gave some traditional answers, something like "helpful, respectful, accessible." Before I could finish, though, the interviewer asked, "Would any of your colleagues say that you're arrogant?" With quick thinking, I responded, "No, they all know that I'm better than they are, but they certainly wouldn't say I'm arrogant."

Sure, that's a pretty arrogant answer. And yes, I have definitely been arrogant at times. (Remember, my second call for my business was a cold pitch to the country's largest financial services company.) But I'd like to think I've gotten pretty good at knowing the difference between arrogance and confidence.

The latter is good. The former can get you into a whole bunch of trouble.

After I made my little arrogance joke, my interviewer laughed. I could tell I had made a good impression.

However, even though I had made that good impression, my attitude changed based on the interviewer's response. Ultimately, I was offered the job but didn't take it. I declined because although I'd be curious enough to entertain the possibility, ultimately, I was self-aware enough to recognize that I would not be a good fit for the role. Sure, the position would have been a step up for me early in my career, but only in the short term. Long term, I knew this was not the right role for me.

How did I know this? In doing my research before the interview, I knew this position had a tremendous amount of turnover, and I also knew, from speaking to others who had left the role, that the person I'd report to (the person interviewing me) was a very difficult person to work with. Some said he was a bit of an antagonist (hence the arrogance question). I was eager to continue in my professional growth; taking the interview was a step in that direction, but I was not willing to significantly change who I was to accommodate this poor leader.

Success does require some bluster and arrogance at times, even if it is only to show other people you mean business. As a leader, you can't come across as weak or meek because no one is going to want to follow you. By definition, a leader is only a leader if there are followers. But if you don't tamp down that overconfidence with humility, the world will eventually give you a healthy slice of humble pie. Knowing the difference between confidence and arrogance takes some level of self-awareness.

Remember, the problem is that generally, those lacking self-awareness don't know they do.

There are people who succeed in sales but can't manage others. Some great athletes make terrible coaches. Some people who are good on their own can't handle marriage or kids. If things have come easy for you before, you may not know what to do when things get hard, especially in a new role.

One way to handle new challenges is to just quit. People do it every day. That's fine if you don't care about your long-term success. It's an easy way out. An even *easier* way—especially if you're looking to go easy on your ego—is to blame everyone else. If you are struggling with this, I suggest re-reading Chapter 3 again.

But if you want to keep going down a path of continued growth and success, you need to be humble. Or get humble. You need to be able to tell yourself, *Man, I'm not prepared for this. But that's okay. I'll Figure It Out.*

Because you can, it's the only way to keep going.

Asking the Right Questions

I know someone who fancies himself as a management consultant. He says he can go into any company, diagnose what's wrong, and tell them how to fix it. He says this, but what's the reality? He goes into a company, points out everything he thinks is wrong, and then leaves, with everyone there hating him. He doesn't care if he's right or wrong. In his mind, he is there only to point out mistakes.

Would it surprise you to learn that despite all of the expertise he claims to possess, his phone never rings?

I call this *seagull leadership*. The seagull swoops in, drops a bunch of shit and then leaves the mess for others to clean up.

What if some guy came into your company and pointed out everything he thought you were doing wrong without asking any questions as if they knew better than you? You would hate him, too. Most of the time, we know what's wrong. We just don't know how to fix it. To have someone point out the obvious, with a smug tone, will make whoever is on the receiving end of that criticism push back even harder. They'll get defensive and double down on the mistakes being made.

Instead, this guy should ask smart, intelligent questions. Often, questions are thought of as a sign of not knowing and, ultimately, weakness, but they can be the most powerful tool for change and leadership.

You don't want to seem like you don't know something, especially if you are in a position of authority. I get it. But a well-placed "Well, hang on a minute, why do we do things this way?" or "Remind me again, why is it that things work this way?" can open up a world of possibilities.

Do not be afraid to question yourself or to challenge yourself. Do not be afraid if someone else challenges you. I don't mind if this happens. It helps me slow down and ask myself: *Should I have done this? What am I missing here?* More often than not, I am missing something. If you recall, I did not land every customer I went after, not right away anyway. But what helped me land each and every company that first told me "No" was my willingness to ask questions. I was not afraid of their feedback, as brutal as it may have been at times. I needed to hear it, and I needed to address it. My ego could only stand in my way, so in order to move forward through learning, I had to put that behind me.

The best leaders I've ever encountered are the ones who are not afraid to be wrong and admit that more input might help. Often, the leader is looking for nothing more than validation that they are approaching the situation in the right way. Allowing the team to provide input ensures everyone is on the same page.

If you want to know what type of leader you are working with, start by listening to the words that come out of their mouth. How often do you hear the words *I, me, my*? Or how often do you hear *us, we, together*? How often do they ask questions and actually engage in a discussion, or how often do they shut ideas down with their own opinion? When someone in a leadership role is asked what they do, do they answer with their title or with an explanation of their responsibilities? When a leader introduces someone beneath them on the org chart, do they introduce them as a colleague or someone who works for them? The leaders who stay humble and put the team ahead of themselves aren't "seagulls" but chameleons. They can adapt and shift as needed. Instead of swooping in and dropping something before leaving, they stick around, blend in, and are right alongside the rest of the team. They ask questions and switch their colors as needed. They become who the team needs them to be rather than who they think they need to be.

Anyone who has worked with me over the years has often heard me say, "Your answers are in your questions, not your statements." Stop saying things and start asking.

Asking questions in this way can also diffuse a tense situation. It shows that you are open to questioning yourself and learning. So many people are focused on being right, being the boss, and, of course, having all the answers. But if you are humble—and effectively humble—that can be the greatest sign of leadership ever.

This works in most situations, even if you are not in a leadership role. When my daughter was younger, she came home once and showed me her math test. She got all but one question right. I congratulated her, as it was an impressive score. I asked her, though, what went wrong with that last question.

"Well," she said, "the teacher didn't teach that one, so I didn't know how to do it."

This got my attention. What teacher would quiz a kid on something they hadn't taught?

"The teacher didn't teach it?" I ask, a little surprised. "Really? No one else in the class got that, right? No one got a perfect score?"

"Well, no. Some kids got a perfect score."

"Ah, well. That's a different story, then," I told her. "It's okay that you didn't get it perfect. But don't say that it's not your fault. It's okay to admit you were not fully prepared for that question. Next time, ask more questions if there is something you don't understand. Don't start by blaming the teacher. Instead, take responsibility and talk to the teacher. The teacher is going to be impressed by you admitting you didn't know something. And you'll be better for it."

If that management consultant had taken this approach and asked the right questions at the right time, I'd bet people would appreciate his ability to listen and discover. They'd become partners with him in both figuring out the problems and the solutions. And he'd probably get more business.

Don't Be the Boss, Be the Example

I once worked at a bank and had a boss who would go around telling people what to do. Fine—that's his job, I guess. But when someone, including the other leaders within the bank, would ask, "Okay, sure, but why?" He'd always give basically the same answer: "Because I'm the boss."

Do you know who is not a great boss? The guy who always has to remind you that he's the boss.

While he may think this projects confidence, it's really just hiding a deep insecurity. Instead of working hard to do a good job and be a good leader, this guy was just using his title to get people in line. That may work for a little while, but ultimately, you'll be exposed for what you are. A fraud.

Instead, you have to have a learning mindset and always try to improve, just like I discussed in Chapter 3 about self-awareness. You won't always get it right, but you'll always be committed to doing your best. If you do this, your employees will see it too. And they'll make the same commitment—and only then can you effectively lead. You won't be the boss. You'll be the example.

When I was in my senior year of high school, I was in a vocational program where I spent the first half of the day working at a factory that made shrink-wrap machines. I worked beside this guy, Craig, who was my supervisor. He was a simple guy with no kids or family. At the time, I was making around $10 an hour. Craig was making probably three times as much or more.

I remember going in every day and just resenting Craig. I could see what we were both doing in terms of output, and I was doing so much more than him while making a fraction of what he did. I couldn't believe it. I was this high schooler doing all the work while this old guy sat back and watched me and the other employees get things done.

Then, after a few months on the job, I realized something. Craig wasn't getting paid for his work. He was getting paid for his wisdom. He wasn't in my face about it because he was humble. He had been working at this factory for thirty years and knew everything about it. If something went wrong, he could fix—in about fifteen seconds—a problem that would take me days or weeks to solve.

Craig's expertise is the same reason a plumber makes $300 an hour (or more) to fix an issue with your sink. Yeah, he's in your house for maybe only half an hour, but don't you think there's a reason you called him in to fix it rather than doing it yourself? As with Craig, the plumber proves a valuable point: knowledge is everywhere, but wisdom is hard to find. Their experience is worth something.

They just do their job and leave. They lead by example.

I led by example in my company in many ways. One way was by telling my customer support people to forward anyone who was unbearably rude right to me. I trained them the best I could, but the reality of any customer support job is that there will always be customers who feel entitled to their strong, if sometimes asshole-ish, opinions. They would send me those customers, and I encouraged them to listen to our conversations.

I wanted them to hear how I handled these situations. They didn't turn into a screaming match, and I never threw my staff under the bus. No one ever shouted or yelled at me when I picked up the phone or raised their voices. Sure, I had a fancier title, and most of our thousands of customers knew who I was, but the real difference was in how I chose to speak. I spoke confidently, I took control of the call, and I guided the customer to the resolution (most issues were caused by their own user error—surprising, right?) Leadership in these situations came in many forms, but it started by ensuring my team knew that I had their back and that if anyone was going to take unnecessary verbal abuse from someone, it was me.

There's more to leadership than what you might see on the surface. In fact, if you see a leader quietly observing and not doing much but talking to people, and then those people knock it out of the park each time, I'll bet this leader is doing much more leading by example than anything else.

As he helped the men's gymnastics team win a medal for the first time in sixteen years at the 2024 Paris Olympics, Brody Malone didn't show much emotion or flaunt his skills. Why? Because his dad told him to "Be humble. You don't have to tell people how good you are. People will know it when they see it."[14] Contrast that with what you might see on the court of an NBA game these days.

When I was a General Agent, being in the office first was important to me. Did I need to be? Definitely not. Sometimes, the only work I could do that early in the morning was to empty the communal dishwasher.

---

[14] https://www.youtube.com/watch?v=BJxTboVkEP0

One day, one of my advisors brought in a potential client early in the morning, and they saw me emptying the dishwasher in the kitchen. The advisor brought the client over and introduced me. He was shocked to see me putting away forks and spoons.

"The owner of this company is emptying the dishwasher?" he asked. I could tell by his tone that he thought this task was beneath me.

"Well, I dirtied them, didn't I? If I made the mess, I can help clean it up."

I don't know if I impressed the client or not, but I knew I was leading by example. My employees knew I was there for them, whatever they needed, even if it was just helping tidy up the kitchen.

Chapter 8: Train Your Body and Mind

Takeaways:

- Don't jump in and expect success.

- You must have good training when it comes to success in business, career, or life.

- Create the right mindset and mental fortitude to overcome any challenge that comes your way.

My wife was a champion high school and college gymnast. She spent most of her adolescence practicing hard, day in and day out. Her training became part of who she is. Even to this day, even though she hasn't competed competitively in years, every time we go to the beach, she'll get out on the sand and hold a beautiful handstand for as long as it takes for me to get a good photo.

On more than one occasion, I attempted my own beach handstand to show my wife and kids that dad can do anything. You will not be surprised to learn that I regularly fell straight on my ass.

A quote attributed to a Navy SEAL goes, "Under pressure, you don't rise to the occasion; you sink to the level of your training. That's why we train so hard."

Now, some version of this quote goes all the way back to the Greek poet Archilochus, who said, "We do not rise to the level of our expectations. We fall to the level of our training."[15] So you know that this isn't rocket science.

But for whatever reason, people still think that if they just jump into the thick of something, unprepared and untrained, they can come out on top. That's bullshit. That is not going to happen. I can try and try those handstands all day long, but I'm still going to end up covered in sand. There's no way I can do what my wife can unless I commit myself to learning how to do a handstand and practicing to the point of perfection.

If you want to Figure It Out, you can't just jump in and expect success. You've got to put in the work to train and learn. Otherwise, you are going to end up covered in sand.

If your success depends on your physical abilities, you've got to train your body. If you want to be a great athlete or reach some kind of personal best in a competition, you better have a training regiment to meet this goal, with key milestones along the way.

But just like you need to train your body for a race or a championship game, you also must train your mind for success. You need to learn how to handle the ups and downs, for which there will be many, so you can create the

____

[15] https://www.linkedin.com/pulse/under-pressure-you-dont-rise-occasion-fall-your-level-christian-bosse/

right mindset and mental fortitude to overcome any challenge that comes your way.

The handstand example may seem simple, but consider the story I told about my old boss at the factory, Craig. His example shows what this kind of dedication to training and practicing can do for someone. Craig spent thirty years at the same factory, making the same product each day. His experience turned into wisdom, earning him the right to work at a different level than mine.

You must have good training when it comes to success in business, career, or life. If you want to Figure It Out on your way to success, you will need to put the time and energy into what you want to achieve. It hopefully won't take you thirty years, but you are going to need to be fully committed if you want to achieve anything great.

Train Your Mind

When I started my technology company, my business partner (who, if you remember, was also my uncle) was a computer programmer. He had essentially zero experience starting or growing a company. But that was okay. That was actually why we worked together well. He had the expertise in programming, and I had it in business. We made a great team. We both trusted each other implicitly because we had to.

At one point, he decided out of the blue that he wanted to "be a business owner." He had always been a business owner on paper but behaved as an employee. Then, he decided he wanted to see himself more as an owner than an employee. For him, behaving like an owner meant being more involved in the day-to-day operations and decision-making rather than being just a software developer. Unfortunately, for him and for anyone looking for an easy way out, you can't just flip a switch and become something you are not.

A big part of his decision to make this switch was meeting the attorney through the regional business association. This attorney knew very little about our business and my partner's role in it and had never even met me, but after an hour-long conversation, this attorney convinced my partner that he was the brilliant business mind the world was looking for. My partner knew nothing about negotiating contracts, handling lawyers, hiring people, firing people, building out various departments— and he certainly knew nothing about what it meant to bear the risk of all these decisions. But he decided he was a business owner one day and was ready for all of it. Imagine if I decided I was a computer programmer that same day; how seriously would he have treated me and my sudden conversion?

Becoming something you are not doesn't happen after a single decision. Sure, you have to first decide what you want to do and what you want to be, but after that, many decisions are made to achieve your goal. Just like how an athlete has to train their body for their sport, you have to train your mind for whatever goals you have. Training your mind can be just as hard as training for a marathon.

The problem for my uncle was not that he sought to take on more than his mind could handle. He certainly could have fulfilled his dreams of being the head person and top decision-maker if he had wanted to. The problem was that he was not committed to the training and the education it requires to truly understand the difference between just doing your job as a programmer, collecting a paycheck, working through the list of tasks someone else gave you, and what I was doing; building and running the business. For him, this training would have required not only a long road of business education but a complete mental shift in how he made decisions and chose to lead people. For example, in 2019 and 2020, when these discussions came up about him taking more responsibility, he was unwilling to stop taking a paycheck twice a month, even though I, as his business partner, hadn't taken a single check since we started the company. The company couldn't afford to pay me while also investing in other areas of the company to ensure our growth. Truth be told, we couldn't afford to pay him either, but without a steady paycheck, he would have been forced to take employment elsewhere. As a "business owner," I decided to forgo my compensation. My uncle did not make the same sacrifice.

The same would have been true for me to learn coding. I could not have flipped a switch, opened up a computer, gone right into our software, and started to code. Although I feel like, given my appetite for learning, I could have learned to code and maybe someday could have been as good as him, but given his thirty-year head start (and my disdain for computer programming), I doubt it.

Instead of asking me for help to learn what it meant to actually run a business, my uncle decided to look elsewhere. He sought advice from the wrong people and relied on their advice as if it was the truth. Instead of doing the work to learn and educate himself and rely on those he knew he could trust, he decided those around him, especially me, did not have his best interests in mind. For years, I spoke to my uncle three to four times every day. We discussed every business decision openly and honestly. Our families hung out on weekends; I left a lucrative position and turned down an even more lucrative one—and even used my own money to help him pay his bills so we could build this company together. After one meeting with a lawyer he had just met, I became the enemy.

This led to the lawsuit he eventually filed against me and the company we created together. Of course, I wish he hadn't done that. But when it came my way, I followed my own advice: I got better training. I worked to train my mind just as I would if I decided to strengthen my body.

I became a law student, not just relying on the advice of my lawyers or what I found online but sifting through it all to figure out what *I* thought was best and made the most sense for me and the company. I am certainly not a lawyer, but I learned enough to know how to handle the situation. I took the advice, lessons, and knowledge from my legal counsel and what I had discovered doing my own research and made my own training course to follow. Most importantly—and one major difference between how we handled our end of the dispute—I spoke for myself and the company and relied on my attorney for legal guidance. My uncle handed the reins for all of it over to a man he had just met.

The FIO Mindset

If someone grows up quitting or blaming others, that becomes their natural tendency. That's their default mindset. This mindset goes unquestioned and unchallenged for many, and these people never truly realize the implications. Remember what I said about those who lack self-awareness, that they don't know it? That's their training—and they remain un-self-aware.

They'll get stuck where they are when something goes wrong instead of looking for ways to improve their training. They'll stay sunk in their dilemma rather than pushing themselves to where they need to be. Often, this means quitting. If the issue is someone else's fault, then there's nothing you can do about it, so why bother? It always seems to be someone else's fault.

When I was nineteen years old, I went to basic training at Lackland Air Force Base in San Antonio, TX. On the first day, I was told I had to fill the "chow runner" role for my 62-man unit. My responsibility was to walk into the dining facility, stand at attention in front of a table full of drill instructors, and say this sentence: "Sir/Ma'am, Flight 421 is prepared to enter the dining facility from the west hall." I had to do this before my unit would be able to eat.

You might be thinking—is that a typo? No, it's not. It sounds like nonsense about an airplane landing in the dining hall, but that's what they told me to say. To the most intimidating drill officers on base. On my first day. I know that was exactly what I said because it's burned into my memory. I will never forget it.

This table of senior officers in the dining facility has a name: The Snake Pit. This happens in dormitories all across the base to break recruits in. You walk up to the table and say what you were told to say, and the drill instructors just lay into you. They yell, they scream, they get right into your face. What they say isn't important—no one remembers what's yelled after it happens. What's important is if you can handle the stress of senior officers tearing into you and follow through with your instructions—repeat your line and nothing else.

It's like playing a very stressful game of Simon Says. The Snake Pit wants you to make a mistake, but you have to not panic, process the information you're receiving (in this case, being yelled at), and stay calm. It's a simplified, heightened version of a scenario many others might encounter as a leader.

Why do they do this? Not because they are cruel, but because they want to test if you can hack it in the military. They want to know right away what kinds of recruits they are dealing with. They also want to ensure each trainee understands that one mistake outweighs a thousand correct answers. In battle, a mistake could mean death to fellow soldiers and civilians. So, you need to be able to follow the simple task of knowing your lines, maintaining your bearings, and addressing someone correctly in a very tense situation. In the dining hall, the stakes are low. But in battle, following directions and protocol can save lives. Testing someone's ability to do this in the dining hall is a simple yet effective way to prove a point.

On the first day, for our first meal, I did just fine. I said my line, and they did what they did. I kept my composure.

Well, meal two comes around, and it's someone else's turn. I go in with him. It did not go as well.

Within a few seconds, the other recruit was in tears. He completely broke down, crying. He could not handle it. I immediately saw that this guy would not get out of his Snake Pit easily.

So I step in. He had his script written down on a piece of paper—the same thing I had to recite earlier—since he hadn't memorized his lines right away like I had. I didn't need a printed script. But he did, which was already one strike against him, opening him up to more ridicule from the instructors. I repeated the statement, just like I had done before. The Snake Pit turned to me. Once again, I took the abuse.

What was my reward? As a nineteen-year-old, one of the youngest men in the unit, I got promoted to dorm chief. That meant I was now in charge of all sixty-two men. Not only was I in charge, but I was also responsible for their actions. If one of them messed up and (for example) didn't make his bed in the morning, when the instructor came around to check, he would get chewed out, but so would I; not exactly what I wanted on day two of my military career. But that was my assignment and my job to Figure It Out.

Now, had I learned some kind of trick to withstand the abuse of a military-level dressing down? Did I read a book or watch some lecture on how to handle four senior officers screaming in your face for minutes on end? No, of course not. There's no education for that.

But you can train yourself to handle anything that comes your way. My training for this moment began as a child, raised on military bases by a military father. Even at nineteen, you would have been hard-pressed to throw me into a situation where I couldn't figure things out without panicking.

This kind of mindset is essential for anyone wanting to be a successful leader. You must have the ability to not panic, to process information in a logical way, make well-informed, educated decisions, and move with confidence and certainty. This kind of mental fortitude is something that you can train yourself to have over time. In the case of the Snake Pit, it was "easy" in that the task was simple: say your lines and take the abuse.

Let's consider the person struggling to lose weight and keep it off. Is this challenge a mental or a physical one? Most people (and the entire dieting industry) focus on the physical challenge when, in reality, it is almost certainly a mental one. Just as we've discussed about setting proper goals, this person now has to train their mind to think, behave, and respond differently than maybe they've ever done their whole life.

They will have to form ongoing habits of success. They must have a commitment to learning. They must know how to run their goals rather than having their goals run them. Above all else, they must know how not to give up.

No doubt, the attorneys who sued me did not expect me to have the FIO mindset. They expected me to give up. They saw this happen all the time. About 90 percent of lawsuits are settled out of court.[16] Knowing this, they expected me to give up.

But I did not have this mindset. I had the exact opposite: Let's go! I got motivated to take these lawsuits on and win. My attorneys were astonished at how much I knew and how easily I grasped what was going on. The FIO mindset is predicated on being proactive.

Mental fortitude is defined as the ability to have strength in the face of adversity. This does not mean you are a mindless, emotionless robot who processes information and takes action without consequence.

During the peak of my lawsuit fiasco, I was juggling three suits, eight different attorneys, nine members of my staff, and a growth trajectory for my company that I could

---

[16] https://hbr.org/1990/01/five-ways-to-keep-disputes-out-of-court

barely keep up with. My company was growing the fastest, just as so many were trying to take me down from all sides.

This was also a time in my life when I was hardly sleeping, consuming only Nilla Wafers and coffee. But most people I saw every day didn't know I was living like this. I kept my emotions inside and just pushed through. I tried to keep things light for my family and my employees as best I could.

You are always going to have emotions. But you need to keep those emotions in check—and process and proceed in spite of them. That's mental fortitude. That does not mean I didn't get angry with my attorneys or the entire environment I was dealing with. What it meant was that it was my responsibility to Figure It Out and move forward. I could have leaned on the stress as an excuse for my behavior or just given up when things got too hard. But excuses don't solve problems.

Whatever situation comes your way, find opportunities to educate yourself and Figure It Out. Slow down the work, compartmentalize the problem, and then recognize what needs to be done.

Take a challenge for what it is. In business, a "no" is not a never, just a "not right now." In getting healthy, a scale that doesn't move is not a plateau but an opportunity to change your routine. In life, a setback is never a step back; it's a step forward in a new direction.

Chapter 9: Don't Just See Opportunities, Take Them

Takeaways:

- Find opportunities in your questions.

- Taking on opportunities means risk—don't be afraid of that.

- Be aware of the dark side of success and the relationships you'll lose along the way.

A friend introduced me to a guy a few years ago. He had come up with a product aimed at improving seniors' health. He had developed the product a long time ago and even applied for—and received—a patent. But he needed some help launching a business around it. My friend, seeing how I was able to build my own company offering compliant text messaging services to financial advisors, thought my experience starting and growing a company could help this guy.

I agreed to speak to him as a favor to my friend. The guy was clearly passionate about what he had developed. He strongly believed that it could help people and make him a lot of money. He saw an opportunity in the market.

The problem was he wasn't willing to take the next step to capitalize on his idea.

Instead, he wanted me to have the same passion he had for his own product. He wanted me to agree with him—saying, "Hey, wow, what a great idea. This is a sure winner." Then, he wanted me to take my commitment to my own idea—the text messaging service—and transfer that same enthusiasm to his.

Unfortunately, it doesn't work like that.

Many people will tell you they have an idea or think that they can solve some gap in the market. They probably can. But many of them don't follow through on their ideas.

Why? Because they are scared. Now, usually, there are a lot more reasons people give besides fear as to why they don't do something, but, in my experience, it always comes back to fear.

This guy, with the medical invention, could have had a billion-dollar idea on his hands. The way he talked about it seemed plausible to me. He was clearly very dedicated to it and very inspired. But we'll never know how much it was worth because he wouldn't pursue it on his own. He wouldn't take the next step. He'd never take the risk to figure out how to keep moving his idea forward.

If you want to Figure It Out to succeed, it's not enough to recognize an opportunity when it's presented to you. You also have to take on the risk of jumping into something new. You have to be able and, most importantly, willing to take whatever steps are required to follow through on the opportunity that's been presented to you.

I knew I had a great opportunity on my hands with my text messaging service when I went to a conference of financial advisors and mentioned what I was doing to a few of them. Soon, people were seeking me out, asking me when the product would launch and when they could sign up. Of course, I was excited to see the enthusiasm from my peers and to tap into a potential market. But I also knew that things would not go smoothly from here. And boy, I was right. Building a business was not simple, and surviving the attacks was even harder, even with a product that everyone wanted.

What I didn't do after that conference was bask in the validation of my idea. That's what the inventor of this medical product did. He had people tell him what a great idea he had and then didn't do anything about it. Instead, he wanted someone else (me) to take on the risk to market and sell it. He didn't have the FIO mindset to take on the opportunity. He just saw the opportunity and felt good about having come up with a great product. But a great product or idea is never enough.

Because I was able to move past the first step of opportunity—recognizing the opportunity when you have it—and on to the second step—taking on the risk, I was able to build a successful company. He continued talking to person after person about his idea, hoping that someone would match his excitement and do the hard work for him.

Find Opportunity Through Questions

Before you can take the risk to capitalize on an opportunity, you must first find the opportunity. The only way I know how to find opportunities is to ask questions.

Asking the right questions serves a lot of purposes. In Chapter 7, I showed how asking questions can help you stay humble. But they can also help you identify solutions or ideas that no one has thought about yet.

The start of my company came when I kept asking the question, "Why hasn't this been done before?" to anyone who knew about regulatory compliance with financial advisors. Many people told me there was no way to send clients a legally compliant text message. I didn't believe them. It did not take me long to realize that the very people to whom I was asking my questions were not inclined to Figure It Out but instead were comfortable with saying, "It can't be done." That was my opportunity.

But these opportunities don't only present themselves in your professional life. There are always opportunities everywhere you look.

In the introduction to this book, I told the story of a friend who got married late in life and was struggling to become a husband and dad. He would come to me to talk about his challenges, but really, he wanted to vent. He wanted to validate his feelings and sit in that validation, just like I could have done when a conference full of financial advisors told me what a great idea I had for a product. What my friend didn't see was the *opportunity* in his situation.

He wasn't asking me the right questions. In fact, he wasn't asking questions at all—or reflecting on who he was in this situation. He didn't ask me, "Derrick, when you first became a dad or a husband, how'd you feel? How'd you figure out how to operate in this new way?" Instead, he was just complaining, talking about how hard it was to have your whole life completely change and be focused on someone else other than yourself. He was just living in willful ignorance. I think it's safe to say that he is not alone in having these feelings and that the list of like-minded new fathers is long—but the list of those willing to share these feelings is probably much shorter.

Because he wanted that validation rather than self-reflection, he missed out on an opportunity to grow and change as a person. He missed out on a chance to become a better dad and husband.

Eventually, he began to Figure It Out, but it took him a while. It would have been a lot less painful if he just asked the right questions. It seems like the hardest part for anyone trying to Figure It Out is to be willing to accept the fact that you are not special. This friend was not facing anything different than any other first-time parent or newlywed, but he was convinced his challenges were unique to him. When I suggested something to him based on my experience or what I knew were the experiences of others, he'd say, "Yeah, but…" and point out why he thought he was different. He wasn't. He just needed to Figure It Out to get his life together.

Asking those questions does open up some vulnerability. Seeking out opportunities means that sometimes you may be wrong in your ideas or you expose yourself to criticism. My friend may not have wanted to admit to me (or himself) that he could be trying harder to be a better dad and husband. He just wanted me to tell him he was right; what he was experiencing was really hard and that he could do nothing about it.

Seeking out that validation, rather than pushing yourself to Figure It Out, is how you get stuck going nowhere. You will have to ask questions and ask for help to take advantage of the opportunities presented to you.

Some see asking questions as a sign of weakness, but the value in the question lies with the one asking the questions, not the one answering them. The right question asked the right way and to the right person, holds within it the pathway forward.

When I started my company, I asked a lot of questions and I asked for a lot of help. I started by asking those around me, who knew more about these things than I did, why exchanging a simple text message with a client was not allowed. Then, when I found out the challenge was strict compliance requirements, I began asking and searching for the next logical step: *Was there a solution out there that was unknown to my compliance team? Or was there literally no solution?* When it became clear there was no existing solution, I decided to solve it myself. That led to my next question: *Could a computer programmer help me design this texting product?* That's what led me to my uncle, who was, in fact, a programmer.

I kept asking questions and figured out my way to the answer. In my case, the answer was starting and growing a company.

That's what made me different from the guy with the medical product idea that went nowhere. That's what can make anyone different.

Opportunity Means Risk

When I decided to write this book, I mentioned to a few people what I was doing. For years, I have heard people tell me I should write about my experience, not only in business but my entire life. To many, my life almost seems like it's so crazy it has to be a movie. When I started telling people that I was finally writing that book, I was somewhat amazed to see how many people I knew who also had an idea for a book.

Most people think they have a story worth telling. But do they actually figure out how to tell the story? Probably not. If you want to tell your story through a book, you've got to sit down, think it through, and do the work of writing and editing. If you actually put in the effort to do this, you may realize that what you have is more of a fireside story, not a book. Just like taking the next step in building a business or inventing a new product, you've got to be willing to commit to the time it takes to do the work.

That's risky. People don't like risk. People are afraid of risk. What you thought was a great product idea could be a dud. What you thought was the next bestseller is really just a fun anecdote for a party.

My wife is very risk-averse. As I said before, she was uncomfortable when I took on the work of the business, as well as the lawsuits. I am not risk-averse at all, maybe to a fault.

So, when I saw the opportunity to start a business, I took it. I knew it was a risk, but I didn't care.

How much easier would it have been for me to stay at the six-figure job I had at the time at a bank? I went to work at eight each morning and was home at five. I punched in, and I punched out (figuratively, of course). That would have been a fine life for me. But how different would my life have been if I had done that?

Risk aversion often means people don't see the opportunities right in front of them. Or, it keeps them from taking that next step of Figuring It Out to take advantage of the opportunities they really do have. Writing a book is hard. It's also scary. Putting yourself out there means that people can tell you, "Hey, I read your book. I didn't like it. Not for me."

But, at least for me, avoiding the risk meant that no one would ever read my story. Even if it's just one person saying it, I'd never hear, "Your book was great. Thanks for writing it."

While talking about starting a business, Elon Musk said, "Starting a company is like staring into the abyss and eating glass."[17] It's hard, messy work. It's uncomfortable and challenging. It's also thankless. Most people don't fully understand or appreciate what goes into starting a company from the ground up.

But to capitalize on opportunities, you must be willing to be uncomfortable. And be willing to take a risk. It's scary. But it's worth it.

Imagine if Elon Musk hadn't become the largest shareholder in Tesla and hadn't chose to take on the risk of building the company. How far behind would we be now with electric cars? And imagine if I didn't write this book? You wouldn't be reading all this wonderful wisdom that will change your life for the better. (Okay, maybe that's my arrogance coming through, but if you made it this far in the book, I assume you've gotten something out of it.)

Capitalizing on opportunities sometimes means making a quick decision and not worrying too much about the risk involved. Immediately after my uncle sued me, he was still working at the company and my business partner.

---

[17] https://www.youtube.com/watch?v=wVmGSMWkS9c

We weren't speaking, but we still had to make decisions together. As you can imagine, this was incredibly difficult.

Of course, this dynamic didn't last long. One day, I received an email from my uncle that included his letter of resignation. I did not mind this, of course, as I knew it would happen at some point, but since he was the lead programming architect of the entire product, his departure would be a real problem. With my uncle gone from the company, I was down to only one engineer, who happened to be close friends with my uncle and came to the company to work with him. I had very little interaction with this remaining engineer at this point, as my uncle was his main point of contact.

I knew that my uncle had already probably spoken with this engineer, and there was a real risk he'd leave, too. If my only remaining engineer also left, I would be forced to basically start from scratch. This was a huge, immediate challenge for me and my business.

But it was also an opportunity. As soon as I got my uncle's letter of resignation, I dropped what I was doing, called the remaining engineer, and told him we needed to have lunch.

He agreed, and over lunch, he shared that, as I suspected, my uncle had already told him his side of the story. What my uncle didn't expect, however, was how prepared I was to illustrate how misguided my uncle was being—and his real goals with the lawsuit. After the engineer saw, with his own eyes, the statements made by my uncle's attorney and the accompanying demands, this engineer chose to stick with me. In fact, as far as I know, after that lunch (where he decided to stay), those two never spoke again. I showed that my support for this engineer had no limit, and he knew that if he stayed with me, we could build a great company together.

He saw the opportunity I was offering him and took it, which was the only reason the entire company didn't crumble that day. I saw the opportunity to share my side of the story with this guy, and it fully paid off.

The Dark Side of Success

When I first decided to pursue building a text-compliant solution for financial advisors, I shared the idea with those in my personal network. Why wouldn't I, even if many of my friends and family had no concept of financial advisor communication regulations? It was something I was excited about, and I never had anything new to talk about. Honestly, how often do we ever really have something new to talk about? As I started to tell them what I was doing, there were so many people who were excited for me. They wanted to hear more. They wanted me to start my company and go on to experience success.

When I took the leap and started my company, and people saw I was actually doing it, I could feel the enthusiasm around me going down. When I'd see my friends, and even some family members, and shared with them how things were going, one thing became crystal clear: the enthusiasm they once had for me was turning to resentment.

At first, I was confused by this change. What had I done to make them annoyed with me rather than excited? Then I realized it had nothing to do with me and everything to do with them. Almost everyone I spoke with (and really, almost everyone in general) had goals for themselves. For many, these goals were better defined as pipedreams because they would almost certainly never come true. These goals had already failed or been put on pause for whatever reason. They wanted so much out of life but chose to settle in the day-to-day monotony that was my old life at the bank. They still wanted and dreamt of so much more but never had the courage to take the risk. Many of these people had their own ideas for products or companies, but those ideas stayed just that—ideas. They resented the fact that I had moved my idea forward and, worst of all, that the results were real.

This is the flip side of seeing opportunities and taking on the risk. People don't talk about this part of success, but it has an impact on your relationships because you are doing what others want, but refuse to do because they are afraid. As we've discussed in earlier chapters, if you want to achieve great things, you're more likely to succeed by surrounding yourself with others who share that mindset. Losing weight and getting healthy is hard to do if your spouse is overweight, unhealthy, and doesn't share that same vision. People tend to gravitate towards those that are like-minded because it's comfortable.

I recently met up with a friend who is a successful financial advisor. I walk into the bar, and he's sitting there waiting for me. He's wearing a baseball cap with "Maserati" written across it.

Of course, the first thing I ask him is, "Did you go out and buy the hat, or did you get the car, and the hat came for free?"

He said he bought the car. Now, most people probably don't want to hear about someone's six-figure car. They can't relate. They're jealous. Not me, though. I asked him all about it. He couldn't wait to tell someone all about his new car, and I couldn't wait to hear.

When you choose the FIO mindset and become successful, you will find people do not want to hear about it. You are going to lose relationships with friends and maybe even family.

That night at the bar, my friend with the Maserati told me that all the friends he had had when he started out as a financial advisor—every single one—were no longer his friends. He spent years grinding to Figure It Out on his way to success. Then, when he had it, people didn't want to acknowledge the work he put in. They saw him as lucky. They resented him for what he had built because they weren't willing to do the work themselves. If you are willing to take the risk and Figure It Out, there will be many people who don't have the guts to do what you did. What's worse, they expect you not to have had the guts either. The easiest thing to find is an excuse; the good news is that these excuses are everywhere if you want to use them. Most people will take those excuses and resent the people who don't.

The Canadian psychologist Jordan Peterson gave a lecture about how you can tell if someone is truly your friend. The key test is if they let you share bad news and listen rather than trying to play a game of one-upmanship with their own bad news.[18] "I got fired," you'd say, and a not-so-good friend might say, "Oh, I remember when I got fired. It was so terrible," and then go into a long story about their experience, rather than letting you share your own.

A truly good friend will also let you share good news and help you celebrate, rather than feeling jealous about your good news and not wanting to hear about it. Peterson says you must surround yourself with people who want the best, for the best part of you. It's not only acceptable but desirable to surround yourself with people who are facilitating your development.

Don't let this deter you from seeing and taking the opportunity. Through Figuring It Out, you learn who in your network deserves to stay in your network. You find out who your real friends are. Real friends are all you really need.

---

[18] https://www.youtube.com/watch?v=k5ukKf4vi6g

Chapter 10: Look for Luck,
But Don't Count on It

Takeaways:

- If you get lucky, use it.

- Put in the work to capitalize on luck when you have it.

There are times throughout my life that I got lucky. Very lucky.

You've probably had these moments too. When things just seem to work out. Or you are in the right place at the right time. You happen to be at the same party as your future spouse. You get a call from a recruiter who has a perfect role for you the day after you decide to quit your dead-end job.

We can all be lucky, just as we can all be unlucky. But what we shouldn't do is think that luck is anything other than what it is. Don't consider yourself particularly special because you got lucky a few times. That's when you get a big head and start thinking you don't actually need to work hard to succeed.

But you should also be ready to take advantage of the luck you get. Just like you need to recognize and follow through on opportunities (as I discussed in the last chapter), you also need to be looking for luck and know what to do with it when you get it.

Doing so can give you the boost you need to overcome whatever challenge you might be facing on your path to Figuring It Out.

Luck from the Start

I was lucky in my life to be born into the family I have. Yes, my upbringing was challenging, but I have never believed that it was a bad thing. My father dropped out of high school to join the Army, and my mother joined him on his journey shortly after graduating high school. They knew what it meant to work hard, save, budget, and make sacrifices. Those traits were passed along to me as a child and shape how I approach everything in life.

Consider the alternative. Because of the lifestyle my wife and I have created, my children are growing up in a completely opposite way. In that way, they are lucky. They are fortunate not to be forced into the same struggles I faced. They are lucky to have parents who can help them while they manage the ever-changing and stressful world they are growing up in. They have technology I would have never dreamed of having and information at their fingertips that no previous generation has ever had.

To those on the outside looking in, my children have privilege, but in my opinion, I had more than them. They are lucky, but their luck is different from mine and comes with its own challenges.

A few years ago, my father apologized to me. I was shocked. He said, "I'm sorry for the way I raised you. I am sorry for being so hard on you and for getting physical at times." I told him, "I don't regret you holding me to those high standards. You may disagree today with how you delivered the message then, but now, years later, what I focus on is the message itself."

The expectations my parents had for me are my privilege. I was so lucky to grow up with next to little in the way of possessions that it forced me to work hard and appreciate what I had. It forced me to Figure It Out, leading me to every other success I've had in life.

My kids have more things and more opportunities than I ever had, and they are not learning the same lessons. It worries me. Kids these days are walking around with cell phones that cost almost $1,000 each, but the struggle required in life to truly appreciate that possession is missing. I worry about their ability to handle the challenges that will eventually come their way. And this isn't just about my kids—it's about their whole generation. Part of why I wrote this book is to offer a different path forward for them and others growing up today.

Luck Throughout Life

To show you what I mean, I'll share three stories of when I got lucky and what I did about it. The first comes from my time in the Air Force. If you remember, I scored very high on the placement test, so I had my pick of the specialty roles. What did I do? I picked the one with the least training so I could get myself back to college and play football. As it turned out, the specialty with the shortest training time, Fuels, happened to have an opening. I picked that one, and off I went.

Well, this also happened to be the most "professional" of the specialties, at least on my reserve base. What I mean by that is I was working with people with a high level of education, often with technical backgrounds, who understood the science and physics of the materials we were working with. In this one unit, I was surrounded by business owners, engineers, and hard-working factory employees. Most of these were the types of people with whom I had almost no exposure while I was growing up.

Because of a seemingly random decision based on a stupid desire to play a game back home, I was put on a path for my career I would have never expected. I saw a whole new world of opportunities before me, and I made contacts that would help guide and mentor me early in my career. When I started as a financial advisor after college graduation, it was this group that I leaned on for advice. For years after my time in the Air Force was done, I would try to return to the base and see this group of people at least once a year.

They loved hearing about my career path. Having the luck to pick a field that I happened to enjoy with a group of men who were so valuable to me can only be described as luck…even though I still don't know why they gave me the nickname of Scooter.

Here's another example: in the early days of my company, I was trying to get in front of as many people as possible. I would make cold calls and get handed off to all kinds of people within the company, like a hot potato no one wanted to land in their lap. I tried to get to the decision-makers in these companies, like the CTO or the COO, but no one would put me through to them.

Then, one day, while researching industry conferences, I came across one for senior investment executives who had published their list of attendees. Many of the decision-makers at my target list of companies were on this conference list. How lucky.

I knew I had to get to this conference. I found the money to pay for it and flew myself there. I was able to introduce myself to all of my targets in person and schedule follow-up conversations after the conference.

After my success at the event, I received a stern letter from the conference organizers that I was not permitted to attend the conference the following year since I had no logical reason to be on the guest list, given I was not actually in a senior position at an investment firm…Oops.

Many of those people I met at the conference became our clients shortly afterward, and eventually, all of them.

One final example: I had a team of lawyers working with me on my federal patent lawsuit. If you remember, one of the three lawsuits I faced was from a competitor claiming that we had infringed on one of their patents. This team of lawyers was very knowledgeable on the topic and had solid people supporting me. But, after three years of facing this fight, I knew that they would not be the team to do it if we went to trial.

Well, as it turns out, we did have to go to trial. So, I asked my attorney, almost as a joke, the name of Minnesota's best intellectual property law firm. Once he told me, I asked if he knew who the best attorney was at this law firm, and once again, he told me. I said, "How great would it be if we could get him to handle the trial?" And again, it turns out that my attorney just so happened to have a meeting set with this guy to connect on a different topic altogether, and he mentioned that he would bring it up.

Lucky for me, this intellectual property attorney had just wrapped up a victory on another case and was more than willing to step in to help. I brought him on as my lead attorney, and the trial began three months later.

These are all examples of what you'd call luck. I was lucky to have this trial attorney free just when I needed him, and I was lucky that my attorney knew him. I was lucky to find that conference list when I did and made it into the conference before they realized I didn't belong. I was lucky to choose a specialty in the Air Force that led me to bigger and better things.

Not only was I lucky, I had done the hard work to position myself to capitalize on that luck. I had performed well on the military placement exam. I researched who I needed to reach to expand my client pipeline and found the conference where they'd be. I had done the work to understand what was required to win at trial, and I knew that my current team of attorneys wasn't the absolute best.

These examples are ones that I look back on with fond memories. However, I can honestly say I had just as much good luck that, at the moment, was disguised as bad luck. Remember the company that called me while I was at Disney World? I was expecting a signed agreement, only to receive a rejection. This phone call, although devastating at the time, changed so much for my company regarding product development, staff development, and even how I presented our solution. It helped me learn how to manage my emotions so I wouldn't get too high or too low when something unexpected came along. These "bad luck" lessons led me to eventually secure this company as a client (and many others). Most people see rejection as unlucky, but when you always view failure as a step forward in growth, any chance to learn is always lucky.

You need to put in the same amount of effort to capitalize on whatever luck might come your way. Do everything you need to do to prepare yourself to be next in line for a promotion so that when, as luck would have it, someone leaves the company, you are ready to go. Make a list of your ideal clients so that if one of them happens to show up at an event, or heck, even at a restaurant, you can approach them with a confident outstretched hand and know exactly what to say.

You have to be looking for luck and know what to do with it when you've got it.

Chapter 11: Persevere with a Purpose

Takeaways:

- Figuring It Out is not about just putting your head down and gritting through whatever may come your way.

- Successfully Figuring It Out means persevering with purpose.

- Figuring It Out isn't a recipe for success by itself. You've got to know what you are capable of and what you aren't.

Imagine you've never fished a day in your life. You don't know the first thing about it. You don't really see the appeal.

Let's say that your neighbor is obsessed with fishing. He does it every weekend and has all the gear. He knows pretty much everything there is to know about fishing.

Your kid comes to you and asks to go fishing. What are you going to do? Are you going to buy some equipment, take your kid to the lake, and figure out what to do when you get there?

That's definitely one option. But you may end up with a pole in the water and a crying kid. Instead, why not ask your neighbor for help? I'll bet he'd be more than happy to give you some pointers and maybe even come along with you to help make it an enjoyable experience for you and your kid. If you are not interested in fishing, why would you put yourself through the torture of Figuring It Out?

There's no shame in asking for help. Figuring It Out is not about just putting your head down and gritting through whatever may come your way. In fact, sometimes that's the stupidest thing you can do. You can end up with a hook in your ass and a broken fishing pole.

When you Figure It Out, you have to persevere with purpose. You have to know what you are good at and what you can reasonably achieve. When you know the obstacles in front of you represent challenges you can't, or shouldn't, take on alone, you've got to either ask for help or consider a different direction.

I had an employee once who, while working for me, was also studying to become a marriage counselor. This shocked me, not because he wasn't a smart, capable person, but because this guy, a recent college graduate, had never even had a serious girlfriend. At that point in his life, his biggest challenge was choosing which bar to go to with his friends on Saturday. He had no real-life experience to be able to relate to his future clients.

Sure, he was more than capable of doing the work and Figuring Out his way to getting his counseling license. Maybe he would have learned enough eventually to support people how they needed it. But without tangible experience, understanding and appreciating the real, raw emotions that couples feel, his advice or guidance would always come from what he learned in textbooks rather than what he actually believed based on experience. Would someone training to be a professional golfer turn to a coach who had never even swung a club? Would an aspiring restaurateur turn to someone for advice whose only experience in a restaurant was as a patron? The answer to both is no. Without real-world experience and an authentic sense of *purpose*, he would find it very difficult to help people how they need it.

Don't Blindly Follow

Figure It Out is all about moving forward. If you've made it this far in the book, I hope you recognize that even when you feel like you may be taking some steps back through some kind of failure or rejection, if you learn from those setbacks, you are actually still moving forward.

However, you can't move forward if you don't know where you are going. I discussed redefining goals in Chapter 6 and the importance of seeing goals as an input rather than an endpoint. But beyond goals—to be certain you are going in the right direction—you also need to know your purpose. Sometimes, this purpose is clear and easy to understand. Other times, knowing what will drive you to success can be challenging. The purpose may not be crystal clear, but, for many, they are confident in the steps they take each day, and that clarity is on the horizon. I had no idea how managing three lawsuits, leading a team, and building a company would play out, but I knew what I had to do each day to keep moving forward. That became my purpose. That's why knowing yourself and being self-aware (Chapter 3) is one of the first things I discussed in this book.

I once lost my job, and I was actually grateful it happened. I should have quit that company long before that moment. However, I didn't know enough at the time to see how my purpose and values were misaligned with the direction of that company.

At the time, I was the Midwest director for a region of a large financial services company. When I accepted the position, my purpose was clear: to help the advisors in my region become better advisors so they could be a better resource for the clients they served. This changed, however, shortly after I started. The company began pushing all of our advisors with unreasonable expectations for selling the company's proprietary products.

When you are an advisor, you want to look out for your client's best interests. This is what I loved about the job. One of the best parts of my role as director was bringing ideas and strategies to advisors solely focused on what was best for the client. But my employer at the time had specific financial products; of course, they wanted to sell as many of those to clients as possible. What was never part of my job description was quickly becoming my only job, and that wasn't what I signed up for.

The company's purpose went directly against my purpose and that of the advisors I worked with. We were trying to put clients first and offer products from any company that would meet their needs; my employer was trying to sell as much of their own products as possible, sometimes even feeling like it was regardless of our client's needs.

Here's what I did: I came clean to my boss about the struggle. I wanted his help in navigating this dynamic, and at this point in my career, when I was relatively new to management roles, this seemed like the most logical first step. I tried to explain the conflicts of interest and how the advisors and I felt about this tension. To my disappointment, he didn't seem to care. In fact, he doubled down on the company's push to sell more proprietary products. He was only interested in what was best for him financially, and I wanted to do what I felt was right. While he didn't say this outright, it became crystal clear to me that I needed to either get on board with this idea or they would find someone else who would.

I tried my best to Figure It Out, but I could not agree with a "product first, service second" approach. It just didn't feel right. The advisors in the field suggesting the products to potential clients began to resent the company. They hated the push to promote products to people. This was right after the 2008 crash, so the pressure to try and turn a profit during a recession was intense. But how could you sell products when you don't believe they were right?

The answer is you can't. So, I was eventually fired. Well, my position was eliminated, but in reality, I was fired. By going to my boss and explaining my challenges, I was essentially offering him the roadmap for firing me. He had all this information on how I was struggling with direction and not meeting expectations. I thought I was going to him with a learning mindset. He saw it as underperformance.

Fair enough. And lesson learned. I should have seen this misalignment of purpose and values long before they fired me and moved on rather than staying and trying to Figure Out my way to a solution that wasn't there. But, as with all things, this was a learning opportunity to understand when to keep working away at something and when to move on.

<u>**Finding My Purpose**</u>

In the summer of 2019, I was the CEO of a growing tech startup, and as a result of years of perseverance, I was finally landing the big fish. It seemed like I was locking down major clients every week. My purpose was clear: be a good leader, a good dad, and a good husband. It was simple but not easy.

Then, at the beginning of 2020, just six months later, I was dealing with three lawsuits, a company struggling to keep up, a significant staff shortage, a severed relationship with my business partner (and uncle), and two young children. Oh yeah, Covid was also just around the corner.

That's when my purpose changed. I had to redefine and refocus so my purpose aligned with what I needed to do. I had to Figure It Out. If I was juggling three balls in the air before—leader, dad, husband—another got thrown at me: law student.

Clearly, I didn't actually enroll myself in law school; instead, I immersed myself in whatever I could find on the subject of my lawsuits to prepare and fight back.

I had to gather all the evidence I could to defend myself while balancing the responsibilities I had before. That's what drove me beyond anything else. If I ever had a question about a decision or the direction I was going, I'd think about whether it was helping me to defend myself in court successfully.

Dropping any of those juggling purpose balls wasn't an option: my company wasn't the only thing being sued. I was, too. The only thing I could do for the sake of my business and my family was to fight back.

I'm more than willing to admit when I am wrong. When I got these three lawsuits, there were a lot of accusations coming my way that I had done something wrong, even illegal. If I was going to say that these accusations were false, I wanted to be 100 percent—or even over 100 percent—certain that I had the evidence to back up what I was saying.

This made me become dramatically over-prepared for what was coming my way. I researched all the claims against me. I gained an in-depth understanding of their legality. If I didn't understand something, I worked with my attorneys until I did. I even found individuals on the other side of the world who could help me with research at a fraction of the cost of my local attorneys so I could accomplish more at a lesser expense.

Then, I put in the work to justify every counterargument I made against my accusers. I was accused of changing our mailing address without notifying my business partner. I found documentation to prove otherwise. I was accused of not paying my partner for his work. I had documentation showing that we had mutually agreed to shift his compensation structure.

I compiled all this documentation in a series of three-ring binders, each about three inches thick. At my first meeting with the attorney for my business partner, before he sued for ownership of the company, I brought those binders and asked him to look through my evidence. Of course, the attorney wouldn't touch them. But those binders were the foundation for how I would respond to the fight he was picking.

I'm a big notetaker. I have dozens of notebooks where I write everything down. After I hit back with the first patent lawsuit, the lawyers for my opponents wanted to look through all of them to help make their case against me. I was happy to share them because I had nothing to hide.

The only problem was that I couldn't find the first notebook from when I originally started my company. I don't know why—it had been so long since then that I had just misplaced it.

This was particularly important for my patent lawsuit, where a competitor claimed that my product infringed on their own patent. Essentially, they said I stole their idea and that I did so knowingly. But this notebook, which they called "Notebook #1," would have refuted that argument because it would show how I came up with the idea in the first place, who I had talked to about it, and how my partner and I approached building our technology.

But I didn't have it. So, my ability to prove myself right—and them wrong—was reduced. However, their ability to prove me wrong was almost nonexistent.

Then, a few weeks before we went to trial, I found Notebook #1. It had been in the bottom of an old box, which I had moved from office to office and house to house. Because we were so close to trial, I had seen all their arguments against me, and I knew this notebook would disprove them all.

When I started preparing and researching for these lawsuits, I didn't know what the end result would be. My purpose was to find data to be able to defend the truth. This was what I believed in deeply, and it kept me going.

I didn't know where I was going to end up, but I just had to keep taking steps forward. And this purpose served me well.

Similarly, if you are on your path, too, you have to believe in that path. You must believe in what you are doing, even if you don't know exactly where you are headed. If you keep your purpose aligned throughout the journey, you'll get to where you need to go.

Chapter 12: Adapt and Move On

Takeaways:

- You can't stop and freeze if you want to Figure It Out.

- Find a way to adapt and keep moving.

- The only thing standing in our way is ourselves and how we think about ourselves.

Mike Tyson once said, "Everyone has a plan until you get punched in the face."[19]

You may have heard that quote before. But not many people know the second part: "Then, like a rat, they stop in fear and freeze."

That second part is even more important than the first. Because, sure, we all know that sometimes we'll get punched in the face. Things are not going to go as we planned. The new job you just earned, with the fantastic team, is never as fantastic as you are told in the interviews. What do you do when you arrive and are met with a list of performance issues on that incredible team that you have

---

[19] https://www.sun-sentinel.com/2012/11/09/mike-tyson-explains-one-of-his-most-famous-quotes-3

to address? Do you walk away or complain? Or do you Figure It Out?

What's important is what comes *after* we take that hit. Albert Einstein said, "The definition of insanity is doing the same thing over and over again and expecting different results." Getting punched in the face, whether physically or metaphorically, and not adjusting is the same idea.

Are we going to stop in fear and freeze? Or are we going to move on?

If you want to Figure It Out, you can't stop and freeze. You'll just keep getting punched over and over again. You've got to find a way to adapt and keep going.

If we make excuses for our actions and aren't self-aware enough to know our true strengths and weaknesses, we will fail. If we want something to fail, it will. Success is possible, but we have to persevere when things don't go as planned. And they never go as planned.

This kind of self-talk can make or break a commitment. The book *Unfu*k Yourself* by Gary John Bishop is all about how we think about ourselves influences who we are and what we do. He makes the point that the only thing standing in our way is ourselves and how we think about ourselves.

So, if you think of yourself as the rat, frozen in fear after getting hit, you are never going to come up with a new plan. You stick to what you know and do not leave your situation.

There's an old saying: if the only tool in your tool belt is a hammer, everything looks like a nail. If your fallback is to blame and point fingers, then don't be surprised when you get punched in the face again. Everything will be an excuse if you've been taught to make excuses. But excuses don't solve problems.

I've learned that the scariest thing most people will do in their lives is to accept responsibility, either for their situation or their own actions. Accepting responsibility is a tremendously humbling experience but extremely difficult. Professional business coaches all over the world make a fortune trying to help people accept responsibility. They will spend hours of your time and thousands of dollars talking to you about responsibility and accountability as if it's a leadership issue. The reality is, in my experience, accepting responsibility is more of a confidence issue. Only the most confident people are able to point a finger inward to say, I made a mistake. There are some elements of leadership in this, of course, but at its core, it's a confidence problem.

These coaches are no different than the weight loss potions and pills that try to sell us something different than what we already know. We already know the solution lies within us, and we have to Figure It Out for ourselves. We don't need outside resources, but we have been convinced it's impossible to change without them. How much do we, as a society, pay to avoid what we don't want to admit?

During the craziness of my lawsuits, my wife told me that a company in Michigan had contacted her about a position they thought she'd be perfect for. For her, this position would be a great opportunity. For me, the timing could not have been worse. Usually, when presented with an opportunity like this, the comfort of staying put generally prevents people from taking the leap. I told my wife to interview for it, and if she chose to accept, I would Figure It Out. Did I want to move my office to Michigan? Not really. Was it impossible to do? Not at all.

My wife did not end up taking the job, but the level of support I offered her is what every spouse deserves.

Here's another example: my family was set to go on a week-long cruise. We'd done a cruise before, and we learned that if we fly in a day early and leave a day after the cruise returns, we won't be rushed if something gets delayed with the ship.

Our ride was set to pick us up very early in the morning, but due to a heavy snowstorm the night before, our flight was canceled, and oddly enough, it was the only flight to Florida that was canceled that day. To pile on, every other flight was completely booked. The earliest we could get out was the next day, which would mean we would not make our cruise. All our planning, excursions, and experiences were now for nothing.

My father-in-law, who did most of the planning for the trip, was extremely upset and wanted to stay home. I, on the other hand, didn't give up. I found a plane to Florida that could accommodate the six of us out of a different airport. We'd still miss our cruise, but we'd at least be in warmer weather. I then began searching for a place that had room for six of us and stumbled upon a gorgeous property in Islamorada. This turned out to be the most relaxing trip at the most exquisite resort any of us had ever been to, so much so that we booked the same trip for the following year.

So far, all of the principles in this book have shown you how to deal with things when they don't go as planned. But what happens in that moment when you realize things are not going your way? Well, you have to adapt and move on.

The trouble is, there's not much I can tell you other than when things don't go your way and you get decked right across the jaw, you have to get back up and keep going.

So, instead of giving you more advice, I'm just going to lay out a few examples to show you what this looks like. Some examples may seem pretty innocuous, but sometimes, the hit to the face might seem like not that big of a deal. You still need to choose how to respond because that's what will keep you on the path to success.

A Presentation Goes Out the Window

A friend of mine was working with three coworkers on a big presentation. She worked for a large financial services company, and her mandate was to show the senior leaders how the company would implement a companywide technology initiative. This initiative was not a small undertaking since it would require updates on thousands of systems, training on new tools, and transitioning away from current technology at a significant cost.

She had clear guidance from her boss the whole time and developed the entire presentation based on what she had been told. It was Tuesday, and the presentation to the senior leadership team was on Friday.

At 2:00 p.m., just as she was putting the finishing touches on the presentation ahead of schedule, she got a call from her boss, telling her that the senior leaders had made a strategic call that was going to have huge implications for the presentation. Instead of implementing the initiative all at once in a comprehensive way, they wanted to roll it out in phases.

At this point, she and her team had been working on this for at least two months, with meetings almost daily to keep them on track. What could she do now?

Option 1: Immediately decide to take the rest of the day off, go to the bar with her coworkers, and bitch about those assholes in the C-suite who don't know what they are talking about. After a few drinks (or a few too many), she would find her way home and then start work the next day with no idea what to do. And probably a bad hangover.

Option 2: Maybe she calls a meeting with her coworkers to talk about what to do, but instead of coming up with new ideas, she complains about what's happening until everyone goes home for the day. Then, she heads home to complain to her family all evening until her husband either agrees with everything she says (to make her feel better) or tells her to move on. She then starts work the next day with no idea what to do.

Option 3: She calls her husband and tells him she will be working late. She takes a breather with her team (maybe even has a beer or two to blow off steam), then starts brainstorming what comes next. She and her team come up with a few good ideas, work on those, and refine the presentation a bit. Maybe she finds that much of the work she had already done still applies to this new scope. She's got a lot more work to do, but she didn't have to start from scratch. She understood that the C-suite that made the change did so with the best intentions for the company, not as a show of disrespect to her and her colleagues.

Obviously, my friend chose Option 3, minus the beer. She came back to work the next day with a clear path forward. She adapted. And she knocked the Friday presentation out of the park.

You Can't Meet Your Sales Goals

You are running a small company, and there's a problem: your sales team isn't meeting its goals.

This isn't uncommon. Happens all the time. So, what do you do?

I'll tell you what a guy I was coaching did, who was in this exact situation: nothing.

I met with him to try to figure out why his department was missing its sales targets. I asked him, "What are you doing to try and turn this around?"

His response? "Everything I've ever known to work is not working."

You'll notice that's not an answer to my question. So, I just sat there and waited for him to continue. He did, saying, "I've tried everything. Nothing is working."

If his department couldn't meet its sales targets, this man was potentially risking not only losing his job but the jobs of everyone who worked for his department. But instead of trying to figure out a solution, he was doing nothing.

He was running a department that needed to adapt and move on, but instead, he's just doing what he's always done. (That's, of course, if we assume that he actually put 100 percent effort into what he had already tried.) He's in a leadership position and needs to adjust, but he only knows what he's always done. When he came up against a new challenge, instead of trying to figure out the solution, he was sitting around hoping a solution would come to him. What kind of example is he setting for his department?

The truth was his team knew he was struggling. He thought that as long as he didn't tell anyone, they would never know he had no idea what to do. But he was asking his team the same questions each week, got the same answers, and was offering no alternatives. His team could tell he was baffled at how to solve the problem.

Consider a combat situation; when twenty guys follow your lead and things don't go as planned. If you do nothing, what happens?

Now, this guy's job, it wasn't a life-or-death situation—although I'm sure his employees would rather keep their jobs. He needed to adapt his plans to this new reality and figure his way out of the challenge.

When I set out to build my company, I did not know anything about technology or what it takes to be a vendor for a large financial services firm. Not only that, but I also did not know the legal structure of building a technology company or even the state-by-state tax implications of a company that does business in all fifty states. Because I had so much to learn, doing nothing was not a path forward. I had to learn, and I had to adapt and move on.

I was having a conversation with someone who had dreams of being an entrepreneur but never found success, and he asked me how I built a successful company. I replied to him, "You're going to hate the answer." I told him I hadn't done anything special, creative, or unique. I told him everything I did was the stuff he and all entrepreneurs know they need to do. The difference was that I did them. While others were struggling with excuses and roadblocks, I was looking for solutions and taking action.

So, here's what I recommended to the guy with the sales company. "Talk to people. Go talk to people who are leaders in similar or even completely dissimilar industries. Ask lots of questions, make very few statements." What I knew he was going to find was although the challenge wouldn't be exact, he was not the first guy to struggle with sales objectives. He was also going to find that, much to his displeasure, no one has a magic secret to solving his problem. He would have to be honest about what he had already tried and how committed he was to those efforts to determine what really didn't work and what wasn't given the time to work. Turning around a sales organization can be like turning around a cruise ship; no matter how hard you pull on the steering wheel, it takes time.

It's hard to imagine this now because everyone has maps on their phone or in their car, but at one point, not that long ago, that wasn't the case. Any time someone found themselves at an unfamiliar intersection, they had to make a choice. They may not have known where the road was going, but they took their best guess, made a decision, and knew they would eventually see something that was either familiar or indicated they needed to go another way. Clarity came after the decision, not before.

Now, people seem to demand clarity before deciding, which is why so many people are frozen when it comes time to make decisions. The answer always comes down to picking a path, committing to it, and adapting along the way. Whether personal or professional, growth is always a slow, evolutionary process, not a revolutionary one.

Focusing on What's Important

The last example I'll give relates to family life, and it's my own. As I've written about this before in the book, I am working on myself. Mainly the emotional ups and downs with my kids—something I know a lot of parents struggle with.

I realized that a lot of my frustrations come when I'm too closely dialed into a situation. I can't get myself out of it and amp myself up unnecessarily.

This happens a lot with my son's sports games. I get too invested, not like that crazy parent we've all seen at these games, but sometimes I get a little too engaged in the game with my own opinions rather than simply appreciating the moment and letting my son have his experience. I felt it was becoming a problem with my relationship with my son, so I decided to do something about it. I adapted my situation to try and move on from this continuous challenge I had with my family.

Last year, when my son started another basketball season, I chose not to be an assistant coach. In fact, I chose not to be involved at all, as a scorekeeper or anything. I chose to sit in the stands and cheer the team on.

Not only that, but I bought a camera to take pictures of the game. I made it my goal not to critique the players or focus too much on the game but instead get really great pictures of my son and his teammates to share with the other parents.

Making this intentional decision to disconnect from the game emotionally helped me adapt to the situation. It wasn't enough for me to remove myself from some kind of official role. I had to give myself a new role. I knew myself well enough to know that without something to keep me busy during the games, I'd fall back into my old patterns.

With the help of my wife and kids, I recognized that, at times, my intensity can be a big problem in my relationships. Together, we realized that this intensity wasn't serving anyone well. I chose to adapt and emphasize strengthening the important relationships in my life. To do this, I realized that I needed to find ways to disconnect my brain in situations that would naturally get my blood pressure up. The camera and the pictures help me distract myself, giving me space to work on what I know I need to work on.

Things aren't perfect. But perfection is not what I aim for. I call it the FIO mindset for a reason. It's not an end goal. If you are committed to Figuring It Out, you are always looking for a solution. You are never going to have the final answer. There are always improvements to be made.

Occasionally, I still find myself getting too involved and a little too excited. This can sometimes lead to tension. But this is less common than it once was, thanks to the changes I've made. I know it will become even less common as I continue to adapt and move on.

Chapter 13: Teach Your Children

Takeaways:

- You can lie to everybody, but you can't lie to the guy in the mirror.

- It's not just what you say but what you do. Actions speak louder than words.

- Surround yourself with the right people; your kids will learn from their example.

As a child, I was very athletically gifted. In fact, just about every team I was on before high school won our championship. I didn't have to go above and beyond; I didn't have to work extra hard or train. I essentially showed up, and we won.

It was good enough while living on military bases, but in high school, after my dad retired and we moved once again to a civilian school, no one cared about my athleticism. Everyone was good. That's why they were on the team. The coaches focused instead on my work ethic. As my athletic career progressed through high school, my playing time went down, and so did my attitude. I can still recall complaining to my parents, blaming the coaches, the kids that grew up in this crappy town we were in who didn't know what they were doing, and the coaches who liked these dumb kids more than me. I never considered there was anything else going on. These excuses also found their way into justifying my poor grades in high school.

After graduation and entering the Air Force, I realized something extremely important. I finally admitted who the real problem was with all my setbacks and struggles: me. I was the problem. Instead of hanging out and emulating the kids who worked the hardest and excelled in both school and sports, I hung out with the people who let me complain. Worst of all, my parents didn't correct me when I complained or pushed me to work harder, which only enabled this behavior. I don't know why this was, but I assume it was because they did not understand what athletics could offer me, not only in terms of potential scholarships but also in creating a habit of focus and discipline. I see now how much I needed my parents to help me see all my complaining for what it was: self-destructive behavior.

The FIO mindset takes a lot of practice. It's hard work. As I always say, it's simple but not easy. You cannot just start doing it immediately.

As with everything, the best time to start learning is when you are a kid. And kids learn the most from their parents' examples. As we reach the end of the book, I want to spend some time on what *Figuring It Out* means for children and the next generation. If you are an adult reading this book, I want you to consider how you can apply this mindset to the kids you are raising.

Because the way they are being raised now does not help them in the real world, I'm not trying to be that classic old fart that talks about "kids these days." Sure, I've got some of that in me. But science proves it: our kids are not being raised in a way that sets themselves up for success.

In his book, *Anxious Generation*, professor and researcher Jonathan Haidt shows how parents have become too protective of their children in the last thirty years. This has led to the creation of the term *helicopter parent*. Kids are not forced to Figure It Out as they navigate through life. In fact, parents think it's best that they do everything for the child. Part of childhood for anyone my age and older was learning from your mistakes, which meant that parents allowed us to make mistakes to some degree.

This, combined with the introduction of smartphones and social media, has created, in Haidt's words, a "rewiring of childhood" for American kids, making them feel more isolated and lonelier. Mental health issues among kids have shot up since around 2010, when the smartphone became more widely available. Many teens report feeling worthless, without purpose, and unable to do anything on their own.

We are spending too much time coddling our children and not allowing them to find their own way. For example, One in four Gen Z'ers have brought a parent to a job interview. About the same have had their parents submit job applications on their behalf. Just over 10 percent admit to having their parents complete HR screening calls.[20]

This would never have happened twenty—or even ten years ago.

And that's a problem because finding your own way is an essential part of Figuring It Out and is probably the hardest parental challenge: letting kids stumble, fall, and pick themselves back up so they know they can do it. This will allow them to handle the challenges they come across when they leave their parents' home and go out into the real world.

If you think I've got some good ideas in this book, start talking to your kids about them. You can help them realize the opportunities in the situations they are in for learning and growth. You don't have to solve every problem for them. This can be frustrating, especially for younger kids, where it would be easier for you to fix the issue yourself. But as they get older, they're going to be much more capable.

Sometimes, You've Got to Be the Jerk

My kids, on most days, don't pack their lunch, charge the electronics, pick up after themselves, or even make their bed. If they were to be asked, my wife and I might get them to do one of these tasks or even all of them. But the

---

[20] https://www.cnbc.com/2024/05/21/gen-z-workers-are-bringing-mom-and-dad-to-job-interviews.html

asking would be required, and they would undoubtedly have some words of displeasure about such a request. When these things don't get done by them, eventually, my wife will give in and just do it for them. I get it. It's much easier than listening to them complain, and with her OCD tendencies, she needs them to be done the "right" way.

My wife traveled often for work and guess what? These same tasks and chores got done. My kids know that if they don't charge their electronics before bed, they will be dead in the morning. They won't have a snack if they don't pack a snack for school. If they don't pick up after themselves, the items they cherish may cease to exist in our house when they come home. (Well, they'll exist, but in the trash can.)

Is this a little harsh? Sure. But, in the case of their missing snack, they aren't going to starve. They'll eat when they get home. Or they'll Figure Out how to get some food at school. What better way to learn about Wimpy, the character from the Popeye cartoon? "I'd gladly pay you Tuesday for a hamburger today." If they're that hungry, they'll Figure It Out. I'm not cruel about it. I'm just clear with them: "If you want to eat a snack, pack it yourself. If you don't, no snack for you."

I've shared stories about how I interact with my son around his sports. Sports are a big part of his life, and this is a direct result of how my parents handled my frustrations with athletics. I was permitted to use excuses, blame others, and point the finger at everyone but me, but the truth is, I wish they had encouraged me more. Sure, I may have pushed back, but as a parent, your job is not to be your kids' friend. It's to help prepare them to be the best person they can be. Sometimes, that requires you to encourage them to Figure It Out on their own, not to allow excuses to be a solution. Of course, the challenge is understanding where the line is between holding them accountable and pushing them.

My kids are twelve and fourteen right now, and, like most kids, they can be quick to blame others or want someone else to solve their problems. They get mad at me when I make them come up with their own solutions. But as they get older, I hope, with time, they will reflect on my insistence they Figure It Out and see how that helped them learn how to be successful on their own.

Because I see what happens when people aren't instilled with the FIO mindset early in life. In so many of the companies I work with, younger employees (and even some older employees) cannot handle the problems that come up. The first example I gave in Chapter 12, about having a presentation changed at the last minute, results in a state of panic that so many people today cannot handle. They just don't know what to do.

Every little thing becomes such a big deal. But if everything is a big deal, nothing is a big deal. On the whole, many people are not wired to look at a problem and solve it themselves. As discussed in the last chapter, they can't adapt and move on.

You Become Who You're With

I came to the principles of Figuring It Out later in life, on my own, partly because my parents didn't encourage me to do more. They permitted my sisters and me to use excuses rather than seek out solutions.

This allowed me to learn habits that taught me to quit, give up, and not expect too much from myself. It wasn't until I left that crappy job changing oil, and really, until I got into the Air Force, that I made a choice to do more for myself and my life.

That's because I was encouraged to be different by the people around me as a young adult and beyond. When I joined the military, went to college, and associated with more successful people than me, I saw attitudes, behaviors, and goals that I wanted to emulate. Who you surround yourself with makes a big difference in the level of success in your life. Oprah Winfrey said, "Surround yourself with only people who are going to lift you higher." If you surround yourself with people who aren't motivated, good luck. If everyone around you gives up, you are fighting an uphill battle every day to break this cycle.

As a parent, you are your child's whole world, especially in the younger years. If you don't live with the FIO mindset, your children are going to feel like they do not have to, either. If you make excuses, they'll see that that's okay. If you solve everything for them, they'll learn that someone else will always fix their problems.

Here is a quick example of this in action: a friend of mine has a child about the same age as my oldest. Instead of basketball, though, his son plays hockey. In Minnesota, where we live, hockey is very competitive. His son, who is a great hockey player, did not make the top hockey team after tryouts.

I happened to have dinner with my friend and his son around the time of the tryouts, and the father listed out to me all the reasons why his son didn't make the top team. These were all excuses. I listened to him criticize everyone involved, with no respect for the kids who did make the team, the process, the coaches, and even the evaluators. What's worse, his son was also invited to participate in the griping.

What lesson was this dad teaching his son? The son walked away from that dinner, convinced that he didn't make the team because of some version of youth hockey "politics." He didn't make it because he didn't know the right people or wasn't friendly with the right kids. The notion that the son could do better, either in the game or in his attitude, was never considered. Attitude drives performance for many great athletes; this kid was no different. Did he have the talent? Yes. Did he have the right attitude to give it his all and learn how to be the best player he could be? Given my conversation with his dad, I don't think so. I was so disappointed in this father and saddened that his son took the wrong lessons away from his youth tryout experience.

When Michael Jordan got cut from the basketball team as a sophomore, his mom didn't complain to the coach. What did she say to her son? "Get in the gym and work harder."[21] He did, and we all know how his story ended.

Take, for example, what my children saw me go through while building my company. When I started, my daughter was six, and my son was eight. Both were old enough to observe what was happening in my life, even if they didn't fully grasp the gravity of it all. When I got served my lawsuits, they did not see me make excuses. What they saw was me working hard. I was in my office when they woke up and when they went to bed. They overheard me at the dinner table talking about whatever challenge I had at the time and what I was going to do about it.

They saw first-hand what Figuring It Out looks like.

I want you to adopt the habits and principles in this book for your own success. But, as a parent, I also want you to do it for your children's sake. I'm sure it will be hard at times, but ultimately, it will be worth it. Your children probably won't thank you in the moment, or maybe even until years later. But I guarantee that at some point, they'll look back and appreciate you for teaching them how to solve problems on their own and encouraging them never to give up. I know my kids will.

---

[21] https://www.basketballnetwork.net/old-school/advice-michael-jordans-mom-gave-him-when-he-didnt-make-high-school-team

Chapter 14: Get Off the Stool

Takeaways:

- Know your meaning of the FIO Mindset.

- The cycle won't end until you end it.

- Keep the inner complainer where that voice belongs.

My grandparents were planners. Many people of their generation were. They jarred their own vegetables for later use; they knew how to use any tool in a toolshed (just in case something around the house broke); they didn't get nice new things because they wanted to save for whatever rainy day might come their way. They thought and planned ahead. Sure, they would rely on others for help, but they also knew how to take care of themselves if needed. If the furnace broke, they could fix it. If a door got blown off its hinges in a storm, they could fix it. Pretty much anything that got thrown at them, they could handle.

Some of this was, undoubtedly, because they were raised on the heels of the Great Depression. That time of scarcity had an impact on their entire generation, teaching people how to fend for themselves and do more with less.

Thankfully, we do not live during those hard times but because of that, we are not as prepared as the Greatest Generation. We live in a time of convenience, where everything is always available to us. We can order food from our phones and have it delivered right to our door, so there is no need to can vegetables for the winter. We can find dozens of specialists online who will come to fix our furnace, so there is no need to learn how to do it ourselves. We can rent any tool we want, so why invest in a toolshed and learn what we can use those tools for?

Living in this time of convenience means the meaning of the FIO mindset has changed. In previous generations, people relied on themselves, their family, their closest friends, and even the church for help. Now, people rely on apps, strangers, and even the government. We are not prepared the way we should be. These changes are reflected in how easily we can slip back into excuses for the problems we face in life: "The plumber didn't show up, so I am stuck with a broken dishwasher"; "The Uber driver was late, so I missed my job interview"; "I don't like the situation I find myself in, so I expect someone else to help me out of it."

If you want to be successful, you need to be able to Figure It Out. If you want to be prepared, you need to have that FIO mindset to tackle any challenge that may come your way. I have seen that people can't get their heads around this shift in their thinking for three reasons: "It's not fun." "It's too hard," and "I don't know how."

I call these the *three legs of the excuses stool*.

I'll go into each of them in more detail, and as you read, think about which leg of the stool you are leaning on the most, preventing you from Figuring It Out.

It's Not Fun

Many people lean on this leg for their excuses. We've been doing it since childhood. If something isn't fun, why do it? When we were kids, we'd rather be playing video games, playing with our friends, watching TV, or literally doing anything else but our homework or chores or whatever we were told we should be doing.

My son and I spent a weekend doing some father-and-son bonding spearheaded by a former Navy SEAL. One of the trainers told us, "Your inner complainer will always be with you, driving along in the car of your life. The question is if you'll let them ride shotgun or not." This *inner complainer* is a lot like your inner child, always telling you to ignore the hard work and make excuses to take the easy path in life.

Instead of putting that inner complainer up front with you, stick them in the trunk. They're always going to be there; you'll always hear them, but they don't have to have any say over where you are going. You can visit them back in the trunk every so often to see how they're doing, but always let them know it's you who is in charge, not them.

The excitement I felt when my uncle and I chose to go into business together carried us through some tough times. However, as you know by now, that excitement wore off not only in our relationship but also in starting a business. It's fun at the beginning, but then it gets hard. Real hard. At a certain point, dealing with all the challenges thrown at the company, even before the lawsuits, was not fun. So why did I do it? My commitment to the company was more important to me, my family, my staff, and my customers than my feelings of having fun at any given moment. Anyone who commits to getting in better shape will tell you that, yes, there's excitement at the beginning of a weight loss journey and a reward at the end, but the middle part is not always fun.

I'm all for fun, of course. You can't live a life of only hard work. But so many people rely on this basic excuse not to get ahead in life. Sometimes, life isn't fun. Don't be afraid of doing things that are hard, and certainly don't use that as an excuse not to Figure It Out.

It's Too Hard

This leg is closely connected to the "It's Not Fun" leg of the excuses stool. We don't want to do things because they take time, effort, or risk. We'd rather keep doing what we've always been doing because we know what that looks like, and it's safe.

Consider the choices I made shortly after barely graduating high school. My parents were hard-working, blue-collar people; neither of my sisters went to college, and my extended family was made up almost exclusively of the same kind of people. Yet somehow, I chose to join the military, not as a career path, but as a means to an end. I chose to leverage the school benefits from the Air Force to pay for college so I wouldn't be saddled with debt, so I could get a degree in a field I was interested in to put me on a path to a different life than my family. This wasn't a better path, just different. The choices I made for myself in no way demean or diminish the choices others have made and how they feel about them. The easiest choice for me was the predictable one right before me. Instead of leaning on my "excuses" stool and saying college would be too hard, I chose the unknown path on purpose.

For many, the "It's too hard" excuse leads to a trap—one of low expectations in your life—low expectations for yourself and others. If you don't think enough of yourself to try hard things, or people don't expect much of you, you'll go nowhere, and the vicious cycle you find yourself in will never end.

Even more, if people know you are one to take the easy way out, they'll take advantage of you. They'll pressure you to do what they want because they know you won't make the hard choices to push back or find your own way to do something. If you don't have a clear path for your life—and a FIO mindset to get you down that path—you'll eventually realize you spent your whole life on someone else's.

I Don't Know How

This leg of the excuses stool is the lamest because it doesn't really apply anymore. We have all the world's knowledge at our fingertips, in our pockets every day. We can learn anything we want about any subject if we just put in the work to learn. You can find hundreds of videos online on how to fix whatever specific problem you have with your appliances. You can find all kinds of instructions and manuals to teach you how to code. You can even enroll in online courses to become a better spouse or parent. As I know from experience, you can also become quite informed on the legal process just by leveraging the world of information available online and elsewhere. I couldn't have done that twenty years ago.

People complaining that they don't know how to do something can reach ridiculous heights. For example, in 2023, Oregon repealed a 1951 law prohibiting self-serve pumping at gas stations. New Jersey still has this law on the books and enforces it. After Oregon repealed this, camera crews parked themselves in gas station parking lots all over Oregon to see how people would handle the change. The results were that many people had no idea how to pump their own gas. Can they be faulted for being nervous about doing something they've never done? No, but they can be faulted for not being prepared. Some camera crews even stumbled upon angry motorists who blamed the government for forcing them to put themselves in harm's way by pumping their own gas.

Because it's so easy to learn something these days, anyone who says that they can't do something because they don't know how is kidding themselves. In almost every case, when someone uses this leg of the stool as an excuse, the real reason they choose not to Figure It Out is because it was too hard or not fun. There's no justifiable way to say that you don't know how to do something these days—or that you can't learn how.

Get Off the Stool—and Get to Work

I am sure you have relied on one of these legs throughout your life, and you may favor one over the other. But now that we are at the end of this book, I hope you can see how leaning on any leg of this stool prevents you from gaining that FIO mindset to help you overcome any problem you face. I'll repeat: excuses do not solve problems.

You can make that shift to the FIO mindset and work your way to success. You just need to get off the stool and get to work.

Conclusion: I'm Not Special

Takeaways:

- Find the rainbow after the storm.

- The journey will not be a straight line.

- You don't have to be special.

After over three years, countless sleepless nights, dozens of boxes of Nilla Wafers, and thousands of cups of coffee, I figured out my way through the three different lawsuits. Two of them—the one from my business partner and uncle and the one from one of my investors—were settled outside of court, and the final one, on patent infringement, went to a trial.

The details of the settlements are not public, but I can say that I never compromised my principles, I never changed my stance to appease anyone, and, while I am not happy about the situation I was in or the expense I was forced into, I am happy with the outcome.

In the public patent trial, however, I can say with authority: I won. Eight trial days, ten-plus hours of me on the witness stand, and two hours of jury deliberation. My attorneys and myself were so prepared that my competitor never had a chance. Not only did I win the lawsuit, but I also exposed their existing patents as flimsy and weak.

That's not all, though: during the years of building this company, I made a lot of great business contacts, and shortly after the lawsuit concluded, I was approached by a prospective buyer for the company. After everything I had been through, I decided that now was the time to sell and move on.

For me, the journey began in 2016 when I had an idea to solve a problem. This journey took an unfortunate twist in early 2020 when I was seemingly attacked on all sides. I ended it by not only fending off those attacks but selling the company and dramatically altering my family's financial position while gaining the freedom to do whatever I wanted for myself and my family from that point on.

I am proud of how I handled myself through these lawsuits, for not giving up, for believing in myself, and, of course, proud of the company I built. The path from aspiring entrepreneur to successful entrepreneur was not straight, but one that was worth it. After reading your way through this book, I hope you also recognize something else in my story: I'm nothing special.

The truth is that most people choose not to Figure It Out on their own. They choose to make excuses, give up, or just don't show up in the first place. Because of this, if you do the bare minimum and choose to persevere, you are already ahead of the pack.

I got served with three lawsuits because the people on the other end, filing those injunctions, thought I'd give up.

The first lawsuit was the patent lawsuit, and the second two were filed by others looking to exploit the stress created by the first one. They thought that a threat of court or false accusations would hurt my ego, and I'd hand over everything I'd worked so hard to create.

Not me. I chose to stick around and fight.

But my choice to Figure It Out and contest the lawsuits wasn't a big decision for me. I didn't sit around deliberating what I should do. I *knew* what I was going to do because I had done it all my life. It was a simple choice for me to push back and not get intimidated. I didn't think about everything that was to come. I just thought of the immediate challenge in front of me: should I fold, or should I keep going?

The answer was, of course, to keep going. Everything else that would come—including my success and the sale of my company—came from one simple decision I made the morning I received my third and final lawsuit. By the time I had closed the door on that normal-looking process server, I had decided to do everything I could to fight these lawsuits. Simple. But not easy.

Everything that came from that decision was similarly simple but not easy. After reading this book, I hope you agree. I chose to share my story—with small tips that anyone can apply —because my challenge with self-help or motivational books is that they are hard to relate to. They are stories of people who do extraordinary, crazy things, and they then tell you how you can be just as amazing or accomplished. Usually, their advice means that you have to completely change your lifestyle and upend how you work.

If you ever meet me, you'll see I'm not unique. I do not seem that accomplished. I'm a regular person. I imagine you are, too. That's why I hope you can see yourself in this book. I hope you can start today with some of the habits I share in this book. You aren't going to be able to take on the FIO mindset in all aspects of your life right away. It took me years. But I hope that you won't take as long as I did and can figure your way to success sooner rather than later.

Figuring it Out does not require massive changes to your life; you don't have to buy anything or switch anything about your routine, at least not right away. You don't have to get rid of anyone in your life unless you want to. I do hope an FIO mindset will cause you to make different decisions in your life because, otherwise, what was the point of this book? But those decisions will come from a new way of seeing the world and a different type of motivation rather than because some successful business guy told you how to live a life just like his.

You can be successful, whatever that means to you. You can define what you want your life to be and work your way to building that life. You do not have to be anything special. I'm not. You just need to work hard and make a commitment to yourself never to give up.

I didn't give up. You don't have to either. You can Figure It Out and find your path to whatever life you want to live. All it takes is a first step.

Appendix: Takeaways

1. **You are in charge of your own motivation; stop looking to others.**

   I set out to change the way advisors communicate with clients with a desire to drastically change the trajectory of my future. It didn't matter what the obstacles were; I was motivated to accomplish both.

2. **Encouragement is a double-edged sword.**

   The right people can encourage you to persevere. The wrong people can encourage you to quit. Surround yourself with the right people. Some people fear challenges and actively look for reasons to avoid them; others see them for exactly what they are: challenges.

3. **Know your strengths and improve upon your weaknesses; be brutally honest about both.**

   I am stubborn and a bit set in my ways, which is both a strength and a weakness.

4. **Perfection is not the objective; improvement is.**

   It's impossible to know what lies ahead. Pick a path, listen, and pay attention. Adapt along the way. Setbacks are never steps back.

5. **Set proper goals.**

In March 2020, winning three simultaneous lawsuits and not losing my company was impossible. Tackling one at a time while moving the company one step forward every day was possible. Your goals are the input, not the outcome.

6. **Get out of the gray**.

Yes or No, Period.

7. **Train your mind.**

Our world is filled with people who are essentially walking speakers, with someone else speaking into the microphone. Become the student once again and embrace learning so you are in control of your path, not simply a blind follower.

8. **Stop letting opportunities pass you by.**

My wife asked me the following question after I sold my company: "Knowing what you know now and how it all ended, would you do it all over again?" My answer was, "Would you want to be married to a man who reminisces about what he could have done or one who shares in the success of what was done? Hell, yes, I'd do it again."

9. **Don't discount luck.**

Luck presents itself every day; take it.

10. Have a purpose; have a why.

Why are you looking to grow/change/evolve/improve? Remember, the "why" won't change, the "how" will.

11. Be a chameleon.

Who I was for my company never changed; I was the leader. How I led, managed the challenges, and interacted with staff and customers changed; success depended on it.

12. Pass it on.

Excuses are a virus and are easier to catch than a cold.

Figure It Out

9 781966 190585